CRUSHED PROMISES

A CHRISTIAN MEDICAL ROMANCE

MONROE FAMILY

LAURA SCOTT

CHAPTER ONE

Dr. Jillian Davis kept her head high, hopefully portraying a confidence she didn't feel as she strode through the emergency department at Trinity Medical Center.

"You're late." Dr. Wayne Netter, one of her colleagues, glared at her from his arrogant stance behind the nurse's station.

She ignored him, refusing to explain she was late because her MRI scan had been delayed. Her personal problems were none of his business. Impervious to his glare, she eyed the list of patients displayed on the large electronic census board. "I see we have a full house."

"There are a couple of trauma victims on the way in," Lacy, the charge nurse, piped up. "Multiple gunshot wounds. ETA less than two minutes."

"Maybe I should stick around, in case you need help." Wayne Netter suffered from delusions of grandeur, acting as if he was the backbone of the emergency department, which is why he could barely tolerate knowing Jillian had been chosen for the role of interim medical director over him. Mostly, she knew, because of his less than amiable personality.

She raised a brow. "Sure, if you like. Although it's Friday night, and I wouldn't want to hold up your plans."

Wayne's gaze narrowed and she imagined he was internally debating with himself. Was it more important she believed he had big plans on a Friday night or that she needed his dubious expertise for two simultaneous trauma victims?

Decisions, decisions. She fought a smile, especially when Lacy comically rolled her eyes from behind Wayne's back. Neither of them particularly cared for the guy.

Clearing her throat, she turned her attention to Lacy. "Any other patient care issues I need to know about?"

"Nope." Lacy shot a quick glance at Dr. Netter and Jillian belatedly realized Wayne might take her innocent remark as something derogatory. The guy's ego was a bit much. She stifled a sigh as Lacy hastened to reassure her, "Everything's fine. Hospital beds are still pretty full and we have a few patients waiting on discharges upstairs."

"Great. I'll head over to the trauma room, then." Jillian walked away, feeling Wayne's piercing gaze boring into her back. To make a bad situation worse, she'd also once turned down his offer to go out for dinner, and he'd been impossible to deal with ever since. He just couldn't believe she wasn't interested. As if he were the ED's most eligible bachelor. Of course, he didn't realize she hadn't dated many men in her lifetime. At first because her mother had been ill and later because she just hadn't found anyone interesting enough.

Wayne did not come close to tempting her. When he didn't follow her into the trauma room, she figured he'd decided not to stick around.

Breathing a sigh of relief, she focused her attention on the nurses and techs scurrying around to prepare the rooms for the incoming trauma patients. Sirens wailed from the ambulance bay and moments later the double doors burst open, spewing chaos into the room.

"Anchor Doe, male, approximately sixteen-years-old with a gunshot wound to the belly, normal saline running wide open through two antecubital peripheral lines." A paramedic called out the pertinent information as the patient was wheeled into the first trauma Bay.

"Evergreen Doe, male approximately the same age at sixteen, was shot in the chest. We intubated him in the field, but his vitals are deteriorating rapidly. Fluids going wide open through two peripheral IVs."

Of the two unknown males, identified by names other than John since that became far too confusing, Evergreen Doe's chest wound was by far the most serious and required immediate attention. Jillian raised her voice to be heard over the din. "Call for a cardiovascular surgery consult, STAT."

"We already did, when the first call about a gunshot wound to the chest came in," Bonnie, one of the trauma nurses, quickly explained. "They were finishing up in surgery and planned to send a surgeon down."

"I don't see anyone yet. Call them again," Jillian ordered.

A nurse stepped away from the bedside to make the call.

"Blood pressure barely 70 systolic and heart rate irregular and tacky at 120," Bonnie called out." Looks like he may be trying to go into a wide complex cardiac rhythm."

Jillian wasn't surprised to see one of the paramedics kneeling on the gurney beside Evergreen Doe, keeping pressure on his chest wound. As the trauma nurses fell into their respective roles on each side of the gurney, she donned sterile gloves and moved closer to examine the severity of the wound.

"Thanks, I have it now." She nodded, indicating he could let up on the wound. A flash of silver on a badge caught her eye and belatedly she realized the man holding pressure wasn't a paramedic at all but a cop.

He released pressure and immediately blood pooled in the center of the young man's chest. The cop slammed his hands back down, covering the gaping wound and leaning his weight over the area. "He's going to bleed to death before the surgeon gets here!"

Jillian couldn't argue—the brief glimpse she'd had of the injury told her it was bad. Really bad. She snapped out orders. "I want four units of O negative blood running through both IV's for a total of 8 units, using the rapid infuser. Get this kid's blood pressure up before we lose him. I also want suction here so I can examine this wound."

Marianne, another nurse, reached up and connected a long clear tubing from the wall suction machine, then handed her the other end. Grabbing a pack of sterile gauze off the instrument table, Jillian turned back to the patient. She glanced up at the cop, registering a flash of recognition as she met his intense green eyes. "Let up on the wound again and this time stay back."

With a grim expression, he nodded.

When he lifted his hands she shoved the sterile end of the suction catheter into the area to clear most of the blood. Using the gauze to soak up the remaining blood, she examined the wound.

"The bullet has torn through the pericardial sack and injured his heart." The injury to the boy's chest was bad, but he had youth on his side. The young could survive a lot more than your average older adult. "Where is the surgeon?"

"He's on the way," Bonnie responded.

"Blood pressure continuing to drop despite the blood transfusions," Marianne informed her in a terse tone. "We'll need to start CPR."

"Give me another minute." Jillian continued suctioning the blood from the wound, and then carefully packed the area with gauze hoping to buy this kid a little more time.

"Dr. Raymond from CT surgery is here," Bonnie announced.

Finally.

"We've lost his pressure!" Marianne shoved the IV tubing aside.

No! Jillian stared at the monitor then glanced down at the young man. "Start CPR."

The cop still kneeling on the gurney placed his hands over the center of the kid's chest and began giving chest compressions. Blood continued to seep from the wound. She didn't waste time telling him to get down—for one thing the strength of his compressions were better than most, and for another, if they didn't fix the hole in this kid's heart soon, their efforts would be futile anyway.

"A bullet punctured the pericardial sac and grazed his myocardium." Jillian quickly gave Raymond the details. "He'll need to go to the OR."

Todd Raymond shook his head as he glanced at the vital signs displayed on the heart monitor. "It's no use. He won't make it to the OR, he's lost too much blood."

Jillian couldn't believe his cavalier attitude. Was he really going to give up that easily? She held onto her temper with an effort. "Are you telling me you're not even going to try?"

He shrugged. "What do you want me to do—open his chest here?"

"Get the chest tray STAT!" Jillian knew their efforts might be useless but this kid was a teenager, for Pete's sake. Didn't this child deserve every chance possible? "Give him some sedation."

When the tray was open and ready, the cop stopped giving compressions and jumped down from the gurney, knowing without being told that his assistance was no longer needed.

The alarm on the monitor overhead beeped loudly as the kid's heart rhythm went straight line without the aid of having CPR. Jillian wasn't a surgeon but she didn't flinch when Todd drew his scalpel down the center of the boy's chest, meeting up with the open area left by the bullet. "Hand me the Macmillan forceps," Todd said as he opened the ribs to expect the damage to the boy's heart.

She did as he asked, but at that moment the fingers of her right hand went numb and tingly, causing her to drop them. For a split second her horrified gaze met the cop's. Good thing the forceps had dropped onto the sterile field. She quickly picked them up again and handed them to Raymond.

"His left ventricle is severely damaged," Todd muttered as he used the forceps to trace the path of the bullet. Jillian crammed more gauze into the blood-filled cavity. "The left lung is also a mess—the bullet tore through the upper lobe."

"Try open heart massage," Jillian said urgently. "Maybe if we can get his blood circulating long enough to get him on the heart lung bypass machine..." She didn't finish. Even she understood that likely wasn't possible. But it would not be for lack of trying.

Todd Raymond did as she asked and messaged the boy's

heart, coaxing it back into some semblance of normal function. But even as they all stared at the straight line where the heart rhythm should have been on the monitor, she knew it was too late.

"It's over." Todd removed his hands from the kid's chest and turned away. "I'm sorry. But with the injuries he sustained, his chance of survival was less than five percent."

He wasn't a percentage, he was a child! She wanted to scream, rant and rave at the tragic death but held herself in check. This boy wasn't the first patient she'd lost and unfortunately, he wouldn't be the last. She opened and closed the fingers of her right hand, trying to shake off the strange tingly sensation. "Thanks for coming down, Todd."

"Sure." The surgeon stripped off his bloody gown and gloves, tossed them in a red trash bag and left.

Jillian stripped off her bloody gloves too, then forced herself to turn her attention to the team of personnel working over Anchor Doe, the first victim. She'd left her senior resident in charge, using her expertise on the sicker of the two patients. "How are things going, Jack?"

"Fine. He's stable. The trauma surgery team is taking him to the OR to repair the damage to his intestines." Jack Dempsey seemed to have everything under control as she watched the surgical residents pack up the gurney and wheel Anchor Doe away.

Good. At least they hadn't lost both of them. Watching one young man die was bad enough.

When she turned back to Evergreen Doe, she saw the cop still standing there, staring down at the kid, seemingly unaware of the nurses who are cleaning equipment out of the way.

When Marianne moved to pick up the remnants of the

boy's bloody shirt and pants, the cop glanced up and held out his hand. "I'll take those."

Marianne glanced at Jillian for confirmation. She nodded, granting her permission. Their hospital policy was always to cooperate with law enforcement when they accompanied a patient to the emergency department. Gunshot and knife wounds were an automatic report to the police, and they had the right to secure evidence. Marianne dropped the bloody clothes in a plastic bag and handed them over. He took the bag absently, staring at the boy, not appearing to be in a huge hurry to leave.

Now that the worst of the emergency was over, she cast through her memory for the cop's name. Alex? No, Alec. That's right. Alec Monroe. He'd come in about two months ago with a serious knife wound slashed diagonally across his flank requiring a good twenty stitches.

Embarrassed at how she remembered his name over the dozens of other patients she treated over the past few weeks, she wished she could slink away, especially knowing he'd taken note of how she'd dropped the forceps. Did he wonder what was wrong with her? Or had he attributed the action to pure clumsiness?

"Thanks for going above and beyond with him," Alec said in a low tone, still gazing at the dead boy.

She nodded. "I'm sorry we couldn't do more."

He raised his gaze to hers, and her heart fluttered stupidly in her chest when she noticed he'd recognized her as well. His mouth quirked in half-hearted smile. "Not your fault, Dr. Davis. He had the best doctor in the state as far as I'm concerned."

She felt her cheeks grow warm and inwardly cursed her fair skin. The cop had made her blush two months ago too, teasing her as she'd stitched his wound. He was tall, well over six feet, and wore his chocolate brown hair short. She remembered his body was pure solid muscle. She'd been more aware of him than had been proper when taking care of a patient.

Opening and closing her hand again, she fought to maintain her professionalism. "I hope your wound is all healed."

"Sure." His smile disappeared. "I only wish these two kids had tried to settle their dispute with a knife instead of a gun. Then this kid might have had a chance."

"I know." She understood what he was saying. Once she would have argued that violence was violence regardless of the weapon of choice. But the crime rate in Milwaukee, Wisconsin had been climbing over the past few years and so had the use of guns. As a result, they treated more and more victims of gunshot wounds, many of them fatal.

Like this poor boy.

"Thanks again, Dr. Davis." Alec flashed a crooked smile.

Call me Jillian. She almost said the words out loud but managed to bite them back. She gave a brief nod instead. "You're welcome."

Alec turned away, stripping off his bloody gloves and taking a moment to wash his hands in the sink before heading for the door. Jillian watched him walk away, hoping she wouldn't have a reason to see him as a patient in the emergency department anytime soon.

Cops like Alec put their lives on the line every day to protect the innocent. To protect the public. To protect people like her.

She couldn't imagine a more thankless job.

Or a more dangerous one.

Yet from the little she'd seen of Alec between this visit

and the previous one where he'd been cut with a knife, he seemed to thrive on his role, throwing his whole heart and soul into his career. Not many cops would have held pressure on a bleeding chest wound like he had.

Jillian shrugged off her troubled thoughts. Tucking her hands into the pockets of her lab coat, she spun on her heel to head back to the main area of the emergency department. No reason to worry about Alec—she had enough problems of her own.

Like how long would she have to wait to hear the results of her MRI?

And did she even want to hear the results?

Her gut instinct shouted no, even though she knew it was better to find out the truth now so she could figure out the potential impact to her career. Her stomach clenched in fear. She knew firsthand, after caring for her mother, just how badly this could affect her future. Although likely not for years yet.

Small comfort.

"Dr Davis?"

Surprised, she glanced over her shoulder. A deep frown furrowed Alec's forehead as he strode back toward her.

Yes?" She pivoted and waited for him to reach her.

"Do you have a minute?" His serious intense green eyes held hers.

Her heart thudded in her chest. She should say no because, heaven knew, the area was full of patients who might need her attention. But she found herself nodding her consent. "Of course. Is something wrong?"

"You could say that. I pulled these out of the kid's pants pocket." Alec's mouth thinned in a grim line as he held the item up for her to see.

"Percocets?" She frowned when she saw the four individually wrapped packages of narcotics. "Was he recently hospitalized?"

Alec cocked his head questioningly. "I don't know. If he was, do medications come individually wrapped like this when you fill a prescription?"

"No." The implication of what he was saying hit her with the force of a ton of bricks. "You're saying these were stolen. Like from a hospital or a clinic."

"Yes." His gaze didn't waver from hers. "Would you know if anyone around here or anywhere else recently reported missing narcotics?"

Jillian opened her mouth and then closed it again without saying anything. Because the answer was yes. Less than a week ago, twelve percocet tablets, just like the kind Alec held in his hand, had been discovered missing from the locked narcotic drawer right here in the Trinity Medical Center's emergency department.

CHAPTER TWO

Alec's stomach clenched as he and Dr. Jillian Davis stared at the individually wrapped percocet tablets lying across the palm of his hand. He'd pulled these out of the sixteen-year-old Evergreen Doe's pocket, and for all he knew the kid had been selling them on the street to other kids. Younger ones. He'd found the two gunshot victims in Barclay Park after all. The idea of a child, like his five-year-old daughter Shannon, finding drugs of any kind made him feel sick.

"We can't discuss this here," Jillian said in a low tone. "Give me a minute to check on the status of our patients in the arena and then we can meet in my office."

Alec gave a tight nod, trying to remain calm. Thoughts of anything happening to Shannon haunted him. He'd only known about his daughter for the past nine months, when Shannon's mother had died and left a letter claiming he was the girl's father and granting him custody. If he had known about Shannon sooner, he would have been a part of her life long before now. It had burned to know Shannon's mother had kept her a secret. Still, he was more than grateful he had his daughter now. Shannon had changed him for the better. He was more relaxed now, less intense.

Less lonely.

He and his daughter—the words still gave him a tiny thrill—had grown close over the past nine months. Seeing kids as victims was doubly hard now. He knew his heightened awareness was due to Shannon. He couldn't imagine anything happening to his daughter.

Shannon was safe for today, in his sister Andrea's care. Andrea was the sensible sibling in the family. Not the wild Monroe, like he had once been. He trusted his older sister with his life.

Shannon was his life.

Swallowing hard, he closed his hand over the evidence bag containing the individually wrapped pills and followed Jillian from the trauma room into the next room. He slid the evidence bag into his pocket and stood off to the side. To take his mind off the seriousness of the situation, he concentrated on watching the pretty doctor in action.

Jillian looked at a computer screen with one of the nurses, no doubt to review a specific patient's medical needs. Alec knew more than he wanted to about how emergency departments functioned. His brother Adam was a doctor and his younger sister, Amber was a nurse, and at one point he'd been trained as a medic in the army with thoughts of following a similar career path.

Unfortunately, healing wasn't his area of expertise.

Maybe that wasn't entirely true, he silently amended. He'd helped to heal Shannon's loss of her mother. When she'd first come to live with him she'd cried all the time, the sound of her quiet sobs breaking his heart. Now she hugged him easily and called him "daddy" without hesitation.

A reluctant smile quirked the edge of his lips.

Maybe Shannon had helped heal him, too.

He fingered the pills through the plastic evidence bag in his pocket. Had the fight between the two teenagers been over drugs? Or a girl? Or something else entirely?

He didn't know. Regardless he couldn't do anything to bring the kid back, as much as he wished he could. Shoving thoughts of the dead teenage boy aside, his gaze followed Jillian's lithe figure as she entered a patient's room.

A few moments later she emerged from the small glass enclosed room and returned to the nurse's desk. His gaze lingered on her, the cute way her forehead puckered in a slight frown as she peered at the computer no doubt reviewing that patient's chart. Her serious expression made him wish he could make her laugh. Her long pale blonde hair was pulled back into a ponytail and he wondered how she would look with her hair down, framing her face.

When he'd been brought to Trinity's emergency department after one of his suspects had sliced him with a knife, he'd been thankful the pretty doctor had been assigned to take care of him. As she'd tended his wound he'd been hyper aware of her dainty capable hands on his skin. For the first time since Shannon had come to live with him, he'd considered asking a woman out.

Thankfully, it had been a fleeting thought. His life was complicated enough, he didn't need to add another element that might disrupt Shannon's newfound peace.

He straightened from the wall when Jillian walked toward him. Despite his mini-lecture, his body responded when he caught a whiff of her scent. Something flowery, but not overpowering. "Alec? My office is this way."

She'd remembered his name. Stupid to be flattered, but he was. She led him to a tiny, compact office without so much as an outside window and waved him toward a seat as she settled in behind the modest desk.

Her medical school diplomas were framed and hung in prominent display on the wall behind her head. The reality of her extensive education punched him in the gut. Pretty as she may be, it was obvious Dr. Jillian Davis existed in a world very different from his.

"May I see those percocets again?" Jillian asked. "I need to check the lot number."

He dug into his pocket and drew out the evidence bag. He tossed it on her desk. "Please don't remove the pills from the evidence bag. Are you planning to see if you can match the lot number to that of the drugs missing from this hospital?"

"Yes, but I'm not sure hospital administration would approve of me discussing the details of that with you," Jillian admitted. She turned over the bag and peered closely at the pills inside. She jotted a series of numbers on a pad of paper. "I think it's best if I get you in touch with our risk management department."

He frowned. He would have preferred to work with Jillian directly. In his experience, once hospital administrators were involved, the lines of communication became convoluted. If not chopped off completely.

He leaned forward, pinning Jillian with a sharp gaze. "Dr. Davis, I don't really have time to mess around with your hospital administration. First of all, it's past seven on a Friday night and I am sure most of the administrative staff has already gone home. If you make me wait until Monday, the trail will be cold. A sixteen-year-old kid died after exchanging gunfire with another, who is right now undergoing surgery. We need to know if these drugs cost this boy his life. Or, even worse, if other innocent kids are in danger."

She worried her lower lip between her teeth and a wave of awareness washed over him. He needed to stop thinking of the pretty doctor as an attractive woman. He had more important issues to deal with than his sudden awareness of a member of the opposite sex.

Not just any member of the opposite sex. Jillian was a doctor, with years of education and training behind her. He'd admired the way she'd managed the situation in the trauma room, taking charge, confronting the apathy of the surgeon on call.

It reminded him of the moment when the forceps had dropped from her dainty fingers. Jillian hadn't seemed like the clumsy type. He wasn't a doctor, but from where he stood it had looked as if she'd suddenly lost feeling in her fingers.

"There are four tablets here," Jillian murmured as she stared down at the Percocet. "A week ago, there were twelve tablets of percocet missing from the narcotic cabinet."

Twelve? Alec forced his attention to the facts she was providing. "So it's not just a couple of pills here and there?"

Jillian shook her head. "No. The time frame from when the drugs were restocked until the time they were noticed missing was almost three hours. At first the nurses thought the pharmacy tech who'd stopped the drawer had miscounted, entering the wrong amount of medication being placed in the drawer by mistake. But when they questioned him, he was adamant he had not made an error. Their nurse who signed off on the tech who'd stocked the drawer also verified the medication was there. A few people went into the machine for medication, but then cancelled their transactions. Management thinks maybe one of those nurses went in to take the pills and didn't record it, but the nurses involved swore they didn't take them and there's no proof any of them did." She shrugged. "For now, the administrators are downloading information from the computer every day, watching for more trends."

"The narcotics are locked in a computerized system?" He grabbed that tidbit of information.

"Yes."

Interesting. He would have loved to see the machine for himself, but that would have to wait. He took a small notebook out of his pocket. "What are the names of the nurses who cancelled their transactions?"

She hesitated. "I really think you should get the information from hospital administration. For all we know someone may have gotten the password of one of these nurses. They could be innocent."

"Okay, then, I'll take a list of all the nurses who are working that day."

Jillian looked apologetic. "The emergency department nurse manager, Rose Jenkins, gathered all the information together for the risk management department. I don't have the list, you'll have to get it from her." His concern must have shown on his face, because she quickly added, "I'd like to help you, Alec, truly. But I really need clearance from hospital administration. There is always a risk manager on call." His nerves tingled when her fingertips brushed against his in the process of handing the evidence bag back to him. "I have to admit, I don't believe this is a coincidence."

No, he didn't believe in coincidences either. As Jillian toyed with her pen, his two-way radio let out a squawk. His partner was no doubt trying to figure out what had happened to him.

He spoke quietly into the speaker and then stood. Jillian —no, Dr. Davis, he quickly amended—glanced up at him. "You need to go?"

"I'm afraid so." He didn't bother to hide the pang of regret. "Would you mind if I called you tomorrow? Are you working?"

"I'm not working but you can always page me, there's a pager app on our phones now and I carry it twenty-four/seven." Jillian rose to her feet and handed him a slim, white business card. "Give me a few hours tomorrow morning to speak with the administrator on call. I'll do my best to help you."

"Sure, that would be great." He stared at the number on the embossed card, understanding her commitment to her job was as deeply ingrained as his. Was she married? Did she have children, too? For some reason, and not just her ringless fingers, he did not think so. "Thanks again, Dr. Davis." He moved toward the door.

"Alec?" The husky way she said his name sent goose-bumps down his arms.

"Yes?" He turned toward her, stealing himself against the surge of awareness.

"Please, call me Jillian." Her smile held a note of uncertainty.

Despite his efforts to keep his distance, warmth seeped through his chest at her request. "Pretty name, Jillian. It suits you." He couldn't help grinning when she blushed. He slid her card into his breast pocket. "I'll talk to you tomorrow."

"Sounds good."

He flashed her one last smile, before walking outside to meet his partner. Deep down, he was looking forward to seeing Jillian again.

Work related or not.

JILLIAN GOT UP EARLY as she usually did and went for a three-mile run. At least her legs seem to be working all right, no sign of weakness there. Afterwards she paged the hospital administrator on call. After she showered and changed, she stood and stared at her closet, desperately searching for something to wear.

When she realized what she was doing, dressing in anticipation of Alec's phone call, she turned away from the dressy clothes and grabbed a pair of comfortable jeans paired with a casual short sleeved T-shirt, her normal attire for her days off.

She probably wouldn't see Alec anyway, unless the hospital administrator returned her call soon. Over an hour had passed and she hadn't gotten a response yet. Likely, she wasn't going to be able to help him after all.

She hoped Alec wouldn't be upset with her. Although why she cared was a mystery. It wasn't as if she was going to see him on a regular basis or anything. Would she? Her heart gave an expectant leap until she squashed the sensation with cold hard common sense. No, of course not. Their paths wouldn't likely cross again.

The tingling sensation returned to her fingers. She stopped in her tracks and stared accusingly at her right hand. The numbness and tingling came and went without warning. Her initial doctor's appointment had been almost six weeks ago. The neurology specialist, Dr. Juran, had ordered a broad-spectrum lab panel, and thankfully the results had come back normal. When her symptoms hadn't returned right away, she'd put off scheduling her MRI scan. Until Dr. Juran had called again, urging her to get it done.

She'd had the MRI yesterday. She'd logged into her computerized medical record but hadn't seen any results. Then she'd called the clinic and had been told the results wouldn't be available until Monday.

Dr. Juran had been noncommittal when she'd asked him about multiple sclerosis. Her mother had suffered from the autoimmune disorder. In the beginning, Angela Davis hadn't suffered much impact from the disease. Yet over time she had grown weaker and weaker until she finally hadn't been able to take care of herself. Since Jillian's father had died of a heart attack when she'd been in her early twenties, Jillian had been left to be the sole provider of care for her mother, until Angela had finally passed away as well.

Jillian caught her lower lip between her teeth. Dr. Juran had explained that MS wasn't hereditary so she needed to stop making herself crazy by thinking she had the same disease as her mother.

With a choppy sigh she flexed her fingers until this sensation passed. Like the first time, the symptoms didn't bother her for long. Just enough to make her aware something was wrong.

She tore her gaze from her hand. Obsessing over a phantom illness was not how she wanted to spend her weekend off. She was lucky to have two whole days off in a row. She fully intended to enjoy them.

And she would. Glancing at her watch, she tried to think of the best way to plan her day, considering all the various errands she had to run.

Maybe she should wait to leave until Alec had called.

Wait a minute, since when did she plan her life around a man?

Not since she'd been sixteen and infatuated with Ethan Wade, the quarterback of the football team who hadn't known the bookworm-school-valedictorian had been alive. The thought made her wince.

With the determined motion, Jillian swept her purse off the counter, intending to head outside. The pager app on her phone vibrated. Despite herself, she quickly pulled it from her purse. The number flashing across the display didn't belong to the hospital.

The hospital administrator calling from home? Or Alec?

She turned and walked back into the kitchen, dropping her purse back on the table. Taking a steadying breath, she pressed her finger on the number flashing on the screen, to connect the call.

"This is Alec Monroe," he said by way of greeting.

Hi, Alec." She placed a hand on her abdomen, willing the butterflies in her stomach to settle down. What in the world was wrong with her?

"Thanks for getting back to me so quickly." His deep voice held a note of warmth, unless she was totally imagining it. "Would you have time to go out for lunch?"

Lunch? She stared off in the distance, imagining her blank calendar. Today was Saturday, and she knew full well she didn't have other plans. She wanted nothing more than to go, but Alec wouldn't be happy to hear she couldn't help him. "I'm sorry, Alec, but I haven't heard back from anyone in hospital administration yet."

"That's all right," he assured her. "I have something else I want to talk to you about."

"You do?" Interest peaked and she quickly gave her consent. "Sure, I'd love to have lunch. Ah, where would you like to meet?"

He hesitated and she wondered if he was about to protest her plan of meeting at the restaurant, insisting on picking her up instead. But she was pleasantly surprised when he didn't. "Do you like Italian? We could meet at Giovanni's, say, around 11:30?"

"Giovanni's is perfect. See you then, Alec."

Jillian disconnected from the call, already shaking her head at her own foolishness. She was acting like a goof.

This wasn't a date. This really wasn't a date.

Ha! Maybe if she told herself that often enough, she'd figure out a way to believe it.

Alec wanted to ask her about something else. Like what? No doubt he had medical questions of some sort. A few of the men she dated in college had seemed to want to know all about various disease processes once they'd known she was a medical student.

She clutched her purse to her chest, feeling the same uncertainty she'd experienced back then, going out on her first date. Yes, as a late bloomer she hadn't gone on a single date until college.

The guy had been nice enough, but their relationship hadn't gone anywhere. In fact, none of the men she dated on and off during college, and in the years since had evoked deep feelings on her part.

Maybe because none of them had been anything like Alec. He was different. He put his life on the line for others, yet oozed masculinity and sensual awareness in a way she'd never experienced before.

She would be lying if she didn't admit that his magnetic attraction made her secretly thrilled to be seeing him again.

CHAPTER THREE

Alec hated working weekends, not appreciating the way the job cut into his personal time with his daughter. He always felt bad when he had to depend on his parents and siblings to help watch his daughter, but then Andrea had mentioned taking the kids to the water park and the excited glint in his daughter's eye had convinced him it was better for her to go with his sister. Beth, Andrea's daughter, was about Shannon's age and the two of them had become almost inseparable over the past six months.

The knowledge should have made him feel less guilty about working on Saturday, but didn't. At least he had off on Sunday, something to be grateful for.

He arrived at the restaurant early, having finished interviewing the neighbors around the area where the shooting had taken place sooner than he'd anticipated.

Standing in the shade of the building, he waited for Jillian, seeking respite from the hot sun. The hours he'd spent gathering information hadn't revealed much about why the two teenage boys had fought, but Evergreen Doe did have a name.

Richard James Borden. Known by his friends as Ricky.

The kid had celebrated his sixteenth birthday three weeks earlier. He'd played football and, according to his tearful and emotionally wrecked mother, had dreams of qualifying for a college scholarship.

Ricky's mother didn't have any idea where he might have gotten the drugs. She claimed he'd been a good boy who hadn't gotten into trouble with the law or skipped school as some of the other kids in the neighborhood did. Football had been too important to him.

He could have pointed out that good kids didn't usually carry guns and percocets but he hadn't. Because deep down he believed her. Ricky probably was a good kid, one who had made the stupid mistake of trying to settle an argument with a gun.

Where Ricky had gotten the gun and the drugs was a complete mystery. Although Ricky's juvenile record did show he once run with a rough crowd. The kid had been hauled in with a handful of other teens for hanging out in Barclay Park after hours. Two of the other kids had marijuana on them. Nothing major, but they'd received a citation just the same.

He glanced up when a blue Chevy sedan pulled into the parking lot. When Jillian climbed out, his chest tightened and he had to swallow past a hard lump in the back of his throat. She was dressed casually in jeans that appeared to have been molded solely for her long legs, paired with the pink V necked t-shirt. In the hospital her long white lab coat and conservative business clothes had given her a professional, hands-off image.

Now, with her pale blonde hair falling around her shoulders, Jillian looked young. Fresh. Beautiful. And close.

Way too close. He wanted to reach out and pull her into his arms. A completely inappropriate thought.

"Hi!" Her breathless smile almost sent him to his knees. "I hope you weren't waiting long?"

He shook his head, trying to convince his lame brain not to fail him, now. He pried his tongue from the roof of his mouth. "Not at all." He stepped up to pull the door open for her, somewhat surprised she wasn't driving something a little more fun and sporty. He could easily envision her in a flashy convertible. "I finished up early."

"I'm hungry," she confided as they were seated at a cozy table for two. "I'm glad you suggested meeting for lunch."

"Me, too". He knew better than to think of a simple sharing of a meal as a date but it was difficult to stay on track when he wanted nothing more than to kiss her. Once they were seated, they pondered the menus and placed their orders. When they both chose the same Italian dish, she laughed.

He sucked in a quick breath. Jillian went from beautiful to stunning when she laughed.

It didn't take much to imagine her smiling and laughing with his family. He came from a loud, noisy clan and he knew his parents and five siblings would love her. He suspected his youngest sister, Amber, especially would get along great with her.

Maybe he should invite Jillian to his parent's anniversary party next month?

No, he already had a date. His daughter.

"I'm sorry I can't be more helpful with your case, Alec," she said in a soft, apologetic tone. "But I promise to make sure you get the list of staff members as requested by Monday afternoon at the latest."

He shrugged, hiding his disappointment. He appreciated her need to go through proper channels, but it wasn't easy to hold off on the investigation when kids' lives were at stake. "That's alright. I wanted to ask you about something kind of related to the case." He flashed a chagrined smile. "Percocets are pain pills."

She nodded. "Yes."

"Can you think of any legitimate reason why a sixteen-year-old would have them in his pocket?"

She sat back in her chair, tilted her head and drew her brows together in a small frown. He liked the way she carefully considered his questions, giving them the importance they deserved. Rather than just shooting off an easy answer from the top of her head. "Not really, unless he recently had surgery, which could be verified on autopsy. But even then, the percocets wouldn't be individually wrapped. Honestly, I have to assume he planned to sell them."

"Yeah." He thought so, too.

"From what I hear, percocets don't have the same street value as other drugs, like oxycodone. And right now, fentanyl is the hottest drug out there." She held his gaze for a moment. "Which makes the situation even more confusing."

He raised a brow at her perceptiveness. "You're right about that. I've asked around and heard the same thing. It's highly unusual for kids to have this kind of drug. Our narcotics division has seen more fentanyl and oxy, along with the usual marijuana, heroin, crack cocaine and meth. Rarely had any of them come across individually wrapped percocets."

Jillian shivered. "I don't like to think about any of those drugs ending up in kids' hands."

Yeah, he was totally in sync with her on that one. The

image of Shannon's innocent smile flashed in his mind as he added a heartfelt, "Me either."

"I guess I've lived a pretty sheltered life," Jillian mused. "I didn't know nearly as much about this sort of thing, other than what I heard on the news until I started working in the emergency department."

Alec found himself wanting to know more about her. He leaned forward. "Did you grow up here in Milwaukee?"

"Yes." She lifted a slender shoulder. "My parents were older when they had me, and they were a bit overprotective. As they were both college professors, I ended up spending a lot of time in classrooms. Not that I minded. I love books."

"I'm sure you were good in school." He could easily see her, studying intently at the library.

"Good enough to be granted a college scholarship." She paused when the server brought their food to the table. "Thank you. This looks delicious."

"Enjoy." The server smiled, then hurried away.

For several minutes they concentrated on their respective meals. Alec glanced at her, his gaze drawn to her lovely face. She'd mentioned living a sheltered life and he could easily see how that might be the case. As far as he was concerned, Jillian shouldn't have to take care of any victims of drug abuse. Which was an entirely unrealistic thought in this day and age. Despite their best efforts to get drugs off the street, substance abuse and narcotic overdoses were on the rise.

He took another bite of his chicken marinara, wishing the ugly side of his job hadn't touched her. No one liked dealing with criminals at any level. Unfortunately, there was little he could do except continue his investigation and then hand over the details to his boss.

Which reminded him of one more thing. "I really need to see your medication dispensing machine up close."

"Stop by while I'm working and I'll be happy to demonstrate it for you," she offered. "The way the machines work isn't a secret. There's no reason you couldn't see how the staff obtain medications from it. And when you get the list from administration, make sure you ask for the names of the staff members who accessed it during those time frames.

"I will. Thanks for the tip." The way Jillian dug into her pasta made him grin. He appreciated a woman with a healthy appetite.

She was beautiful. Successful. Financially secure. He hid a grimace. She probably made at least three times as much money per year as he did. If not more. She was way out of his league.

What was he doing, spending time with her like this? There was no point of satisfying his urge to see her again. No matter how much he might want to. Easy to imagine taking out to a fancy restaurant for a nice, quiet dinner. Followed by a romantic walk along the beach of the lakefront.

His phone rang. He glanced at the display and then flashed Jillian an apologetic smile.

"Excuse me, this is my daughter." He accepted the call. "Hey, munchkin, what's up?"

"Daddy!" Shannon shrieked in his ear. "I slid down a water slide and my whole head went underneath the water!"

A flash of panic made him tighten his grip on the phone. "Are you alright? Are you hurt? Did you cry?"

"No, silly." To his relief she giggled. "I just held my breath. I didn't like it when the water went up my nose, though."

Swimming lessons, he thought, relaxing his fingers the death like grip on the phone. His daughter needed swimming lessons, and fast. "You're supposed to blow air out of your nose so the water doesn't come in."

"Eww. Gross." He chuckled, imagining the scrunched expression on her face. "Oh, Auntie Andrea is calling me so I have to go, Daddy. I love you."

His throat tightened. After years of not knowing his daughter even existed, he knew he'd never, ever get tired of hearing her say that. "I love you, too, Shannon. See you later." He cleared his throat as he pocketed his phone.

Jillian stared at him on her eyes wide with shock surprise. Then she seemed to pull herself together, although he noticed her smile was strained. "Your daughter sounds adorable. How old is she?"

"Five. Almost six." He tried to think of a way to explain without going into the whole complicated story. "She has only lived with me for the past nine months, since her mother died. I just found out about her, then."

"Oh, I'm so sorry." Her expression softened. "That must have been very difficult."

"For Shannon more so. Thankfully, kids are incredibly resilient. She seems to have adjusted fairly well. So have I. We make a pretty good team."

She glanced away, making him realize he'd given the impression that he wasn't interested in expanding that team.

A truth he hadn't meant to state so bluntly.

She reached for her water glass but as she lifted it, the glass slipped from her fingers and fell back onto the table. The glass didn't break, but some of the water slashed over the edge. "I'm such a klutz!" Her cheeks were pink as she leaned over to mop up the mess, avoiding his gaze. "And, actually, I'm sorry but I need to get going. I have a number of things I need to do today."

He couldn't let her go, not like this. Reaching across the table, he caught her hand. "Wait."

She froze, staring down at their joined hands. Then she looked up at him, her gaze uncertain. "For what?"

He couldn't prevent himself from stroking a thumb over the soft skin of her hand as he held her gaze. "You dropped the forceps last night and now this. You are not a klutz. But you certainly seem upset. I hope you don't mind me asking, but is something wrong?"

There was a long pause, but then she tugged her hand from his. "I honestly don't know. But really, I do need to go. Please, excuse me." She picked up her purse. "Thanks for lunch, Alec. I hope you hear from hospital administration soon so you can find the person you're searching for."

Without giving him a chance to say anything more, she hurried away. His gaze trailed after her, and he felt bad about how she'd pulled away from him. He also couldn't help ruminating over what was wrong. She said she didn't know but, as a physician she must have an idea.

He signaled for the check, sternly reminding himself that Jillian's medical problems weren't any of his concern. He needed to stay focused on finding the person stealing percocets from the hospital and placing them in the hands of children.

No way was he ready for anything on a personal level. He'd silently made a promise to himself, not to disrupt Shannon's life. Especially after the way her mother had died forcing her to live with him, the father she hadn't known.

Keeping that promise meant staying away from the beautiful Jillian Davis.

JILLIAN SPENT the rest of her weekend trying to wrench the image of Alec talking to his daughter out of her head. She had thought him an attractive man before she'd known about the little girl. It had been a bit of a shock to find out he was a dad, but seeing him in his sensitive caring mode had made prying him from her mind even more difficult.

Reading professional medical journals helped to a certain extent, because there was always so much to learn. After a couple of hours though, her mind drifted back to Alec. Annoyed, she considered calling the emergency department to see if they needed additional help. Anything was better than sitting around, dwelling on her lack of a personal life.

Especially when the void hadn't bothered her up until now.

When her phone rang early Saturday evening, she was surprised and just a little disappointed when the caller was one of her colleagues, Craig Bartlett.

"Hi Craig. What's up?"

"Hey, Jillian. I need a favor."

"Sure." At the moment she would have agreed to almost anything. "What do you need? Someone to cover your shift at Trinity?"

"Sort of. Trinity Medical Center and Children's Memorial Hospital are sponsoring the Festival of the Arts down at the lakefront this weekend. I'm supposed to be volunteering in the first aid station tomorrow, but my son is sick. Would you mind taking my shift from one to four in the afternoon?"

"Of course." Manning the first aid station didn't sound too hard. Besides, she didn't mind volunteer work.

"Thanks a lot." Greg sounded relieved. "I owe you."

"No, you don't. Seriously, this isn't a big deal. It sounds like fun. Take care of yourself and your son."

"I will."

The next day Jillian headed down to the lakefront early, so she could make sure to find a parking spot. The Art Museum was a beautiful modern white structure overlooking the shore of Lake Michigan. There were various art displays set up along the lakefront and she took a few minutes to browse through the works by local artists before heading over to the small trailer with the universal Red Cross on the front.

A man and a woman stood inside. The guy looked familiar. He stepped forward with a welcoming smile. "Hi. Can I help you?"

"Yes. I'm Dr. Jillian Davis, I'm here to cover Craig's shift."

"Ah, that explains it. I didn't think you were Craig." His green eyes twinkled. "I'm Adam, and my shift is over." He glanced at the woman standing beside him. "Mary, would you mind giving Jillian the rundown of how we're set up?"

"No problem." The woman offered a cheery smile. "My name is Mary Drover, and I'll be here all day."

"Better you than me," Adam said with a laugh.

Mary rolled her eyes. "Go on, get out of here. Thanks for helping out." Mary turned to her. "When I'm not here you can get in touch with me via this phone number." Mary tapped a large piece of paper with a phone number printed on it which was taped to the top of the table.

"Nice meeting you, Jillian. See you later, Mary." Adam gave them both a little wave as he left the trailer.

Mary spent a few minutes showing her around. The trailer was set up very much like a mini emergency room.

Plenty of supplies to care for minor injuries all the way up to broken limbs.

"Alright, I'm going to walk around outside for a while." Mary pointed at the sign. "Call me if you need me."

"Sure thing." Jillian nodded. She hadn't known what to expect from the first aid station, but alone in the trailer, she looked around and thought maybe she should have brought something to read in order to keep busy.

It turned out her optimism was premature. Within ten minutes she heard a little boy crying and a young mother rushed in, clutching a little boy in her arms, her blouse smeared with blood. "My son Joey fell and hit the back of his head on the pavement."

"Okay, let's take a look." Jillian patted the exam table, indicating to the mother to set Joey, who appeared to be about five or so, down. "Did he lose consciousness at all?"

"No. He just started crying." The woman looked as if she might dissolve into tears, too.

The boy was still crying and she tried to soothe him as she examined the back of his head. "There, now, Joey, it's alright. I know your head hurts, but you're fine now." Thankfully the cut was relatively small, but there was some tissue swelling. She took a moment to check his pupils, which he didn't like, but then stood. "I don't think he'll need stitches." She glanced at his mother. "But there is a small lump back here and I'd like to apply a cold pack."

"No stitches? Are you sure? There was so much blood!" The woman cradled the boy next to her to ease his crying.

"Head wounds bleed a lot, but we'll use the cold pack first and see how it goes." Jillian smiled at the boy as his sobs quieted to small hiccups. She cracked a cold pack and mixed the chemicals contents to activate it before placing it gently against the back of his head. "There now, you're so brave. How would you like a lollipop? If your mom says it's okay," she quickly amended.

"That would be fine." Joey's mother appeared relieved when her son stopped crying and chose a grape sucker. "Thank you. I'm glad this isn't serious."

"Not at all, he should be fine." Jillian wondered if most of the patients she'd see during the afternoon would be children. She didn't mind. Sometimes kids came into the Trinity Medical Center's emergency department by mistake, instead of going over to Children's Memorial Hospital, which happened to be located next door. She wasn't a pediatrician by trade, but she could handle kids if needed.

Her next patient proved her theory wrong, when a frail elderly lady came in, after nearly fainting in the heat.

Jillian managed to get the woman to drink some Gatorade and took the time to thoroughly assess her to make sure she wasn't having a stroke or any other undiagnosed illness. She kept the woman lying on the exam table for well over thirty minutes. By then, the woman claimed she felt much better.

"Okay, you can leave, but I want you to head straight home. And if you become light-headed again, call 911, okay?"

"I will, dear." The elderly woman patted her arm. "Thank you."

The trailer was quiet for another twenty minutes before the door opened again.

"Jillian?"

She was just as surprised to see Alec, holding a young girl whose heart-shaped face was streaked with tears. "What happened?"

"Shannon's arm swelled up from a bee sting." He gently

set his daughter on the exam table.

"Is she allergic?" Jillian reached for another cold pack quickly activating it.

"I don't know." He looked worried. "She says she's never been stung by a bee before. I thought we needed to come here in case she needed epinephrine."

Smart thinking on Alec's part. She smiled at the little girl. "Hi, Shannon, my name is Dr. Jillian." The girl's sobs quieted to small sniffles. Gently taking Shannon's arm, she examined the large reddened area right above her elbow. "Do you remember what happened?"

"A bee flew near my juice box." Shannon's tone indicated she despised the creatures. Jillian placed the cold pack over the swollen area, raking her gaze over Shannon in search of other signs of an allergic reaction. The little girl's breathing appeared good, and there were no sign of hives breaking out on her skin. "He wouldn't go away, the next thing I knew my arm burned like it was on fire."

"And you're sure you've never been stung before?" Jillian pressed.

"I'm positive." The little girl's head bobbed up and down. Her dark brown hair was the exact same shade as Alec's but the similarities stopped there. Shannon had big brown eyes, not sparkling green ones.

"I believe you. Alec, the epi-pens are in that right hand drawer over there. Maybe grab one, just in case." She continued holding the cold pack on Shannon's arm, as Alec crossed over to find the epi-pens.

She wrapped a comforting arm around Shannon's shoulders. The little girl's slipped sideways, leaning her head against Jillian, as if the whole traumatic experience had worn her out.

She smoothed her hand over Shannon's hair, catching a

whiff of baby shampoo. Alec's daughter was a cutie.

The thought of having a child of her own flashed in her mind. Then she gave herself a mental shake. She couldn't even think like that. Not when she still didn't have the medical answers she needed.

"What do you think?" His brows were pulled together in a frown as he brought over two epi-pens. "Is she allergic?"

"Not that I can tell. So far, so good." She flashed a reassuring smile. Carefully, so as not to dislodge Shannon from resting against her, she lifted the edge of the cold pack to assess the swelling. The reddened area was already starting to look a little better. "We should keep an eye on this for a little while, yet." She waved at the container of lollipops. "Do you mind if she has one?"

"No of course not." He gave his daughter a curious look. "What flavor would you like? Cherry or grape?"

Shannon lifted her head from Jillian and pursed her lips. "Cherry is my favorite."

He looked surprised but nodded. "I like cherry too." He peeled off the wrapper and handed it to her.

She popped the sucker into her mouth. "Thank you," she mumbled, her speech garbled from the lollipop.

"You're welcome." Watching Alec with his daughter, she remembered how he'd mentioned they had only been living together for the past nine months, since her mother's death. She could only imagine how terrible that must have been for such a young girl.

"Why does cold make swelling go down?" Shannon asked.

"Ah, that's a good question." She tried to think of a noncomplicated answer. "When you hurt yourself, your body tries to fix the injury by sending white blood cells to the area. And while that is good, lots of swelling hurts, too."

The little girl scrunched up her forehead. "Doesn't the body know better than to send so many white blood cells?"

She had to laugh. "No, not really." She lifted the corner of the cold pack again, keeping an eye on the clock. They'd been there for a good fifteen minutes without any worsening symptoms. "Here, see how much better it looks? The cold makes your veins close up and helps the body stop sending so many white blood cells to the area that hurts."

Shannon peered at the sting site in her arm. "Doesn't hurt as much now, either."

The cold pack had probably numbed the area. She glanced at Alec. "You may want to give her some Benadryl tonight, before she goes to bed. The antihistamine will help counteract any bee serum left in her system."

"Benadryl," Alec repeated with a frown. "Okay, I'll have to stop on the way home to buy some."

She opened drawers to check if there were any samples. When she found a small packet of Benadryl, she handed it over. "Here you go."

"Thanks." He stepped closer to take the medication in his unique musky scent drifted towards her. Suddenly, the small trailer seemed even more cramped, his broad shoulders taking up more than a little space. Now that Shannon's minor emergency was over, Jillian didn't know what to say.

Small talk had never been easy for her. She was more comfortable with books.

"Well, I think it's probably time that we head home, right munchkin?" Alec asked.

"No!" Shannon pouted. "We didn't get to spend hardly any time in the children's tent."

"Children's tent?" She wasn't sure what the little girl was talking about.

"I received tickets to come here today from my older

brother, Adam. He told me they have a children's tent where the kids can do finger painting and other artsy stuff."

Adam? She quickly made the connection. "Oh yes. he was here as one of the volunteers. I thought he looked familiar."

"I missed him? Figures." He glanced down at his daughter. "Are you sure you want to stay?"

Shannon pulled the sucker from her mouth. "Yes, Daddy." Then she plopped it back into her mouth and gave a vigorous nod for emphasis.

Removing the cold patch, she took one last look at Shannon's arm. "The swelling has really come down. If you want to stay to enjoy the children's tent, she should be fine."

"Okay then." Alec glanced at her. "Thanks again." He paused and then added, "How long are you working?"

"Another few hours or so." She was deliberately vague.

He nodded. "Maybe we'll see you later."

"Sure." She knew he was just being polite.

Shannon nimbly jumped down from the exam table. "Bye, Dr. Jillian."

"Bye, Shannon. Have fun in the children's tent."

Alec took his daughter's hand as they left. He was a good father. And why that had suddenly become an attractive trait in a man was beyond her. Alec obviously cherished his daughter and the feeling was mutual.

Her memories of her own father were mostly centered around doing homework. He'd always been willing to help, showing great patience when it had come to her studies. She had been an only child, and her parents had been in their early forties by the time she'd been born. They viewed education as being critically important. Most of the kids her age had younger, more active parents, but Jillian hadn't really minded. She'd loved books and once she'd hit high school had fallen in love with science. She'd known then she was destined to become a doctor.

Her choices, sacrifices some would say, had never bothered her before. There was no reason for them to nag at her now. Her career was something she'd worked hard for. Having a family of her own just hadn't been a priority. Especially after her mother had gotten sick and her attention had been focused on caring for her mom, rather than having a personal life.

Now she couldn't help but wonder what she might be missing. When Shannon had rested her head against her shoulder, she'd been struck by a flash of tenderness for the motherless little girl. Never had she been so tempted to gather a child into her arms for a big hug.

But Shannon was Alec's daughter, not hers. And she had bigger issues to deal with right now. Better to stay focused on her health than pining for something she couldn't have.

At the end of her shift, Jillian stepped from the trailer to find Alec and Shannon walking toward her. Alec's gaze was warm as he acknowledged her with a nod.

"Just in time. Are you hungry?" His eyes twinkled. "We were thinking of having barbecued spareribs for dinner."

She tried to come up with graceful way to decline, but then nodded. "I'd like that. Ribs sound great."

They wandered over to where the food vendors were lined up along the edge of the art festival grounds. Eating while talking wasn't easy, although Shannon didn't seem to have nearly the same problem as she chatted about their activities in the children's tent.

After they finished their impromptu meal, Alec insisted on walking her to her car. Shannon danced between them, which made her feel a little bit like they were a family. The minute that thought landed in her brain, she shook it loose.

Don't go there, she silently warned.

"This is your car, right?" Alec stopped next to her blue Chevy.

"Yes. Good night, Shannon." She smiled at the little girl.

"Night, Dr. Jillian." The little girl smiled widely, then abruptly yawned and rubbed at her eyes.

"Have a good evening, Alec." She purposefully kept her tone light. "Thanks for dinner."

"Anytime." He met her gaze straight on and a sizzling awareness flashed between them. The glimpse of desire in his eyes convinced her she wasn't alone in this. Not that it mattered. She could not, would not take their friendship any further. "I may stop in to see you tomorrow."

"Really?" She hoped she didn't sound as juvenile as she felt.

"Yes. You know, to get the list."

"Oh yes, of course." He was referring to the list of staff members she'd promised him, after getting clearance from the hospital administrators. This was work related, nothing more. She unlocked her car and opened the door. "That's fine. I'm working day shift tomorrow."

"Oh." Was that disappointment clouding his eyes? "Then I might not see you. I'm working second shift."

It was tempting to offer to work a double shift, just so she could see him. But she managed to hold back. "Well, thanks again."

As Alec and Shannon walked away, she couldn't hide keen sense of disappointment.

She'd run into Alec today by chance. By once he had his list, she likely wouldn't see him again.

CHAPTER FOUR

Jillian headed to the hospital bright and early the next morning, despite her restless night. It was all Alec's fault, she thought, feeling cranky as she walked in. Reliving those precious moments she'd spent with Alec and his daughter had made it impossible to fall asleep.

Wishing for something she could never have.

At least ignoring her fatigue was easier once she began seeing patients. What she loved most about the emergency department was the wide variety of illnesses and injuries. She was never bored—how could you be when you never knew what your next day would bring?

Just before noon, one of the nurses, Susan Green, gestured her over. "Dr. Davis, you need to look at this patient. He suffered a pretty severe second degree burn on his arm."

"I'll be right there." Jillian quickly washed her hands before walking over to see the patient. She quickly logged into the computer at the foot of his bed, to take a look at his name, brief medical history and his vital signs. Then she moved around to introduce herself. "Mr. Perry, my name is Dr. Davis. What happened? How did you burn yourself?"

"I was stupid," Mr. Perry admitted, grimacing when she lifted the edge of the cold towel to assess the damage. "I was trying to burn some garbage and as it rained the other day, everything in the fire pit was wet. I thought I'd use a little lighter fluid..." He sucked in a quick breath when she lifted the towel all the way off and the air hit his raw skin. "Like I said, I was stupid. There was a small explosion. I dropped and rolled in the grass, then went to stand in a cold shower. Then came here."

"Very smart," she told him. "Exactly the right treatment for a burn."

"Yeah, smart." Mr. Perry, a well built man in his forties, snorted. "Not smart enough to avoid a dangerous shortcut."

"Maybe not, but this could be worse," Jillian admitted. The burned area covered almost the entire expanse of his arm between the elbow and his wrist. "You still have hair follicles, which means you won't need a skin graft. This burn will be painful, but once the area has healed, it shouldn't leave a scar."

"That's good." He managed a wan smile.

She replaced the cool towel. "I'm going to have one of the nurses wash this up and put a dressing over the wound. We'll give you two percocets for the pain. You'll need someone to drive you home, though, if you take the medicine here."

"I'll hold off on the pain medicine for now. Otherwise I'll to call my ex-wife." Mr. Perry sighed heavily. "She won't be happy with me."

Jillian flashed a sympathetic grin. "I understand, but burns are painful. You may need to swallow your pride and call her."

"Dr. Davis?" Lacy poked her head into the room. "You have a call on line one."

She gave her patient one last smile, then crossed over to grab the phone. "Hello, this is Jillian Davis."

"Jillian, Dr. Juran here. Do you have some time you could come and see me? It's lunch time, so I thought you might be able to take a break. I'd like to discuss the results of your MRI scan."

Dr. Juran? Good grief, she'd forgotten all about her MRI results. Her stomach sank to her toes. She momentarily closed her eyes and braced herself. "I guess this means you can't tell me over the phone."

There was a slight pause. "No. I don't want you to worry," he added, "I would really rather see you in person."

His attempt to lighten the blow wasn't working. Knowing her fate was about to be sealed, she forced herself to speak. "I can come now, if you have time."

"That's fine, I'm in my office."

"I'll be right there." She hung up and let Lacy know she was leaving.

"Are you okay?" Lacy's eyebrows lifted in concern. Her distress must be evident on her features.

"I'm fine," Jillian lied, not wanting to go into the whole story right now. "I won't be gone long. Page me if you need something."

Despite her apprehension, she hurried to Dr. Juran's office. She didn't wait for more than a few seconds before being escorted in.

He rose to meet her. "Jillian, please sit down."

She did, mostly because her knees went weak.

He resumed his seat and held her gaze. "Your MRI was normal. However, you need to understand there is still a small chance you could have multiple sclerosis or some other auto-immune disorder.

Wait. What? Her MRI results were normal? The flash of relief faded all too quickly as the rest of his statement sank into her brain. "A small chance? Like how small?"

"Five percent." Dr. Juran, a fatherly man in his late fifties, took one of her hands reassuringly in his. "I would like to do one more test, Jillian. Evoked potentials."

She tried to keep her expression neutral but inside her stomach clenched. "I heard they're painful."

He gave a solemn nod, his gaze apologetic. "I won't lie to you. It is not a comfortable procedure. We can't give you medication to relax you because the purpose of the test is to stimulate the nerves. We can't take away the pain."

"I understand." She stared at him. "Do you really think there's something wrong with me?"

He didn't answer for a long moment. When he did, his tone was gentle. "Jillian, as a physician yourself, you're aware there is still so much about the body, specifically the nervous system, that we don't know. Obviously, you have symptoms that are being caused by something. Let's not think the worst. I've told you before, multiple sclerosis isn't genetic. It's caused by a virus that settles for some reason in the myelin tissue surrounding your nerves."

"Yes." She knew that much. She'd read everything she could about the disease when her mother had grown ill.

He squeezed her hand. "Please, try not to worry. We'll run some more tests and keep an eye on you. As long as your symptoms don't get any worse, there's no need to panic. At this point, your symptoms are mild enough to hold off on treatment anyway."

She took a deep breath and let it out slowly. He was right. She was making this situation worse than it needed to be. "Alright, I will try not to worry. Five percent is a pretty low number."

Dr. Juran flashed a smile, his teeth white against his dark skin. "That's the right mindset. Go out and check with my assistant. She can get you scheduled for your evoked potentials. It will take a week or so to get you in," he warned. "So be patient."

"I will. Thank you." This time would be easier as she really wasn't looking forward to the uncomfortable test anyway. After a few minutes for his assistant to fit her into the schedule for Tuesday the following week, Jillian gratefully returned to the emergency department.

One her way, she stopped in the cafeteria to grab something quick to eat for lunch. She finished her sandwich in less than ten minutes and returned to the arena.

A familiar name on the electronic census board made her frown. Her burn patient, Mr. Perry, was still in his room. The dressing wouldn't have taken that long so why was he still here? She went over to poke her head into his room.

"Mr. Perry, I'm surprised you're still here."

"It's my fault." Susan spoke up quickly. "I realized he was overdue for his tetanus shot, so I gave him that first. Then I was called away to help another nurse. I'll get this dressing done right away."

"It's fine." Mr. Perry waived his good hand. "I'm okay. Although I might take you up on that offer of pain medicine."

"Of course." Jillian glanced at Susan. "Why don't you give him two percocets first? I'll get them ordered in his chart." She turned to the computer and quickly entered the order to cover the nurse pulling the narcotic out of the machine. Then she looked at her patient. "Mr. Perry, I can't let you drive. You'll need to call someone to come and get you."

"I know." He sighed and pulled out his cell phone. Jillian quickly wrote her medical assessment note in his chart listening while he explained to his ex-wife why he needed a ride. "She's not thrilled, but she's coming to get me." He lowered his phone and tucked it back into his pocket.

"Good." Jillian finished her note and logged off the computer. Glancing at the clock, she wrinkled her forehead. Everything seemed to be moving slow today. "I'll see what's taking Susan so long to get your medication."

"I'm not going anywhere," Mr. Perry grumbled.

Jillian stepped out of his room, pulling the curtain closed behind her. She frowned when she noticed there were a group of people crowded around the medication dispensing machine.

"Susan? Did you get Mr. Perry's percocets?"

Susan disengaged herself from the gathering of nurses and shook her head. "I'm waiting for the pharmacy to send more."

Jillian bit back a flash of irritation. "Why? I thought the machine sent a message to pharmacy requesting a restock once the last dose was taken?"

"Yeah, that's the problem." Susan's face was as red as her hair. "According to the inventory there is supposed to be sixteen percocets left. But I didn't find any. They're all missing."

ALEC and his partner Rafe Hernandez were called out to the hospital moments after their evening shift started. He knew, even before Rose Jenkins had told him, that there must have been another diversion of narcotics from the medication dispensing machine.

After he and Rafe walked into the emergency department, they were met by the charge nurse, Lacy, who escorted them to a conference room, her expression grave. "They're waiting inside."

Walking into the room, he scanned the people gathered there and found Jillian. Her face was pale and her forehead was creased in a deep frown. He wanted to offer a reassuring smile, but didn't.

He and Rafe took their seats at one end of the table. Introductions were quickly made—Rose Jenkins, the nursing manager, Jillian Davis, the medical director of the emergency department, Margaret Strauss, Trinity Medical Center's Risk Manager, and Dr. Chris Donnell, chief of staff. All of Trinity's leadership was present and accounted for.

Rose gave a brief summary of the newest discrepancy. Sixteen didn't sound like a lot, but Alec knew that in the wrong hands, it could still be deadly.

"I need a list of all the staff members who are working during both narcotic thefts," Alec said.

Rose nodded and handed him a sheet of paper. "We've gathered the names, twenty-two in all, of those who are working during the time frames in question. The first two nurses on the list have disciplinary action in their personnel files—you may want to start with them. The five nurses with stars by their names were the ones who accessed the machine close to the time frame of the diversion. Upon questioning them, several claimed they hadn't been to the machine, despite the computerized record, making us wonder if the thief is stealing and using staff passwords."

"The thefts also occurred during change of shift, a chaotic time when people are too busy to notice details," Jillian added, her face still pale.

"You don't have security cameras over the narcotic dispensing machine?" Rafe asked.

"No. But in light of recent events, perhaps that's a step we will now be forced to take." Rose Jenkins glanced at the other administrators in the room. "I'm being told by human resources though, that the nurses must be told that there is a camera there. We cannot video record them without their knowledge."

Hmm. Alec glanced at Rafe. He would have preferred a hidden camera but understood he had little say in the matter.

Jillian shifted in her seat, looking as if she wanted to say something, but didn't.

Alec understood why she was upset. "I know it isn't easy, suspecting one of your own to be stealing narcotics. I would still ask that you think about the people on this list and let me know if anyone has been acting differently lately. Sometimes a change in behavior is a clue that there is something more going on."

Jillian's troubled gaze slid from his and he knew her name, along with twenty-one others, was on the list. He didn't believe she was guilty—what could possibly be her motive? Yet he couldn't afford to ignore her as a suspect either.

"Is there anything else we can do to catch this person?" Rose asked.

He didn't have a good answer for her. "Is there a way to take all the narcotics out of the machine? Maybe force the staff to get them personally from a person?"

Rose and Jillian looked horrified.

"No!" Rose shook her head vehemently. "Our patients often need pain medication—we can't go without any narcotics. And forcing one person to get them from another is just not feasible. We see too many patients every day for that."

"Besides," Jillian added, "using the machine gives us a record, even if it's not entirely accurate."

He hated to admit she had a point. But that led him right back to the need to have a secret hidden camera.

"We could ask for all the staff members to take a mandatory urine sample to test for drugs," Margaret, the risk manager spoke up. "Our policy allows for random drug testing."

Rose frowned. "I would hate to put the entire group of staff through something like that based off what is likely one person's actions. It's not random if the entire group of staff members are forced to succumb to the test."

"It's possible our suspect isn't taking the medication for themselves but for someone else." Jillian's gaze locked on his for a moment. "The drug tests would therefore be inconclusive."

Alec jotted a few notes agreeing with Jillian's assessment. The fact that he'd found individually wrapped percocets in Ricky's pocket meant the drugs were probably being sold on the street. "Rafe and I need to interview all the staff on this list."

"Good idea." Dr. Chris Donnell, who had been very quiet during this discussion, finally spoke up. "I expect you to let us know if you find anything."

Alec nodded. "Would you rather have me talk to the staff here at the hospital or down at the station?"

There was a long pause, before Rose said, "Down at the station might be better. That way, the rest of the staff won't know whose names are on the list. It's going to be tense enough around here until we find this person."

"Okay. I'll take care of calling them and setting up the interviews." He took the list of staff suspects and folded it into his pocket. "Anything else you need from us?"

"No. We've instructed all staff members to change their passwords. We'll also continue to look for suspicious trends in accessing narcotics." Rose paused, then offered a wan smile. "We appreciate your help." Rose stood and he followed suit, rising to his feet as well.

He could feel Jillian's gaze on his back as he headed for the door. The leadership at Trinity must respect her position as the medical director to have included her in the meeting. Obviously, they didn't consider her a serious suspect. He glanced back over his shoulder, wishing there was a way to reassure her that he believed in her innocence as well.

He tried to tell himself he believed she was innocent because of her integrity and the way she cared so much about her patients and not because he was attracted to her.

JILLIAN DROVE HOME, her stomach in knots as she tried not to think about how her name had ended up on the list of suspects.

Maybe she should go and volunteer to be interviewed. Surely she'd feel better once she'd gotten that part over with. Would Alec interview her himself? Or pass her along to his partner? And really, what difference did it make?

None. After sharing dinner with Alec and Shannon, she'd allowed herself the brief fantasy of thinking there could be something more between them. But that was before things had changed. Before she learned she still needed another test to rule out the possibility of having multiple sclerosis. And before there was another narcotic theft during her shift.

Alec had no choice but to view her as a suspect. She was grateful Rose and Chris had allowed her to be a part of the meeting. She took her role as interim medical director seriously, would have loved to keep the position permanently.

She was innocent, but it still didn't look good to be linked as a suspect in the investigation. At least the hospital was working with the police. She trusted Alec's cool, logical brain would get to the bottom of these missing narcotics.

The more she thought about it, the more she realized it would be better if she volunteered to have her interview with the police first, setting an example for the rest.

Cranking the steering wheel, she maneuvered the car through a one hundred and eighty degree turn and headed back to the freeway. Thanks to the rush hour traffic, the trip to the fourth district police station took twice as long as it normally should.

When she pulled up in part in front of the police station, a flicker of doubt crept in. Was she making a mistake?

No. Squaring her shoulders, she gathered her courage and marched into the police station. When she asked to speak to officer Alec Monroe, she was politely told he was out on a call.

Of course he was. She should have known cops didn't sustain jagged knife wounds from sitting behind a desk. She should have waited for him to contact her.

She turned away, ridiculously disappointed because she'd really wanted to get this interview over with. Not just because of how she felt personally towards Alec, but because her career was at stake.

"Excuse me? Ma'am?"

She paused, glanced over her shoulder and raised a brow. "Yes?"

"Would you wait for a few minutes? Officer Monroe just called in. He's on his way back to the precinct."

"Sure."

She dropped into a plastic, uncomfortable chair, gazing about with interest. Having never been inside a police station before, she was curious. The place didn't exactly look the way it was portrayed on TV. When Alec walked in, her heart gave a betraying thump of awareness. When he flashed a smile that brightened his eyes, she sucked in a breath.

Oh, boy. Who was she kidding? This was definitely personal.

"Jillian," he greeted her warmly. "What brings you here?"

"I—uh..." She hesitated, glancing around for his partner. "I thought it would be best to get my interview done right away. To set an example for the rest of the staff. If you have time, that is."

His smile dimmed and she couldn't help feeling her reason for being there had disappointed him. "I need Rafe to do your interview, since we've gotten to know each other on a personal basis."

"Yes, that makes sense." She swallowed, feeling awkward. "Is Rafe around? Or is he busy?"

Instead of answering her question, he stared at her for a long moment. His intense gaze made her all too aware of how impressive he looked in his dark blue uniform. It seemed as if he wanted to say something but wasn't sure how to say it.

"This is a bad time, isn't it?" She flashed a weak smile. "I'm sorry. I shouldn't have come unannounced. I'll wait to hear from you or Rafe on the interview."

Before he could respond, a woman ran into the police station, crying hysterically. Alec jumped protectively in front of Jillian, facing the woman.

"Ma'am?" He put one hand out, the other hovering over his gun, as if anticipating an attack. "Calm down. Tell me what's wrong."

"My son is missing. You have to find my son!" The woman was a wreck, sobbing and repeating herself over and over. Jillian couldn't blame her. She'd be out of control if her son was missing, too.

"Okay, try to remain calm. I promise to help you." Alec stayed in front of Jillian. "All we need is a little more information. What's your son's name? How old is he?"

The woman took a very deep breath, then her eyes rolled backward in her head as she crumpled to the floor.

What in the world? She followed as Alec rushed forward. Without saying a word, they both took up a position on either side of the woman's supine body.

"Do you have a pulse?" Alec asked.

She shook her head. "We need to start CPR."

As he had the other day, Alec immediately began doing chest compressions. She pulled a resuscitation mouthpiece out of her purse. Ever since the first time she'd had to do mouth to mouth on a victim, she'd carried one for her own personal protection. The protocol for CPR did not require mouth to mouth resuscitation any longer but since she had the device, she may as well use it.

The officer behind the desk hurried over. "I already

called 911 for an ambulance. Is there anything else you need?"

"Do you have an automatic external defibrillator?" Jillian asked glancing up at him.

"Nah, we don't have anything like that." The guy rubbed a hand over his bald head. "Stuff like this doesn't happen here."

Clearly it did, but that didn't matter. Jillian stared down at their patient. The woman was young, in her late forties. Too young to have had a heart attack.

Alec continued performing chest compressions. She knelt across from him, watching and waiting for the exact moment to give a rescue breath.

"Excellent compressions, I feel a nice strong pulse."

He grinned and nodded not interrupting his rhythm or his counting. She was impressed by how quickly he jumped into medical situations, as if he was a paramedic instead of a cop.

An ambulance siren shrilled loudly outside. In record time, Jillian thought. She stared down at the patient, giving required breaths and thinking the woman must have had some sort of underlying heart arrhythmia that had been exacerbated by stress. What else could have caused the abrupt change in her condition? Especially at her young age?

When the paramedics rushed through the door, Jillian gave orders. "I'm an emergency medicine physician. Connect her to the AED. We need to see if she requires a shock."

Since she still wore her lab coat and name tag from Trinity, they didn't question her authority. Within moments Alec stopped compressions just long enough for the two wide defib patches to be placed on the front and back of the woman's chest.

She watched the screen, noting the woman seemed to be in V-fib. The AED's mechanical voice rang out. "No pulse detected. Deliver a shock."

Jillian pushed the button herself, delivering the shock. It took a moment for the woman's heartbeat to return on the screen. The shock had brought the woman out of V-fib, although her rhythm was not regular. She felt for a pulse, finding a weak thready beat.

"Start a couple of IV's and give a bolus of lidocaine. The way she went down, I suspect she has some underlying heart arrhythmia and went into V-fib as a result of her stress."

Alec rifled through the woman's purse, pulling out her driver's license as Jillian and the paramedics prepared the patient for transfer. When he caught her watching, he flushed.

"I'm sorry, but she said her son is missing. I have to go out and track down someone who can give us the information we need to find him."

"I understand." A missing boy was certainly a priority. She stood. "Can I do anything to help?"

"No, but thanks." He smiled but seemed distracted.

"Hey, Monroe, that army medic training of yours has been coming in handy."

Jillian glanced in surprise at the officer behind the desk.

Alec shrugged. "Thank the government. Your tax dollars paid for my training." He handed him the driver's license. "Pull up this address for me kind of see if we have anything on this family."

Alec had been trained as a medic. No wonder he was so good at jumping into medical situations in the field. She helped the paramedics lift the woman onto their gurney. "I'm sure you two can take it from here."

"You bet, Dr. Davis." One of the paramedics flashed a cocky grin as they wheeled their patient away.

She lingered, watching as Alec continued speaking in a low tone to the officer behind the desk. Obviously, she wasn't needed here. As she turned to make her way towards the door though, he caught up with her.

"Jillian, I have to run, but I'd like to talk later."

"Sure. I'll give you pager number." She was about to rattle it off, but he shook his head.

"No need, I have it memorized. I'll call you," he said as they parted ways.

She lifted a hand to wave, unable to voice a response. Her insides had gone all soft and mushy, like a popsicle sitting in the sun on a hot summer day. Hearing that Alec had taken the time to memorize her number temporarily rendered her speechless.

CHAPTER FIVE

"Daddy?" A small soft palm gently but insistently patted his cheek. "Daddy? Are you awake?"

Not even close, but obviously his daughter was. Early mornings wouldn't have been a problem except for the fact that he worked second shift. And last night he hadn't gotten home until much later than usual, well after midnight. Thankfully, Megan, the college girl he'd hired to stay with Shannon while he was working, didn't mind. Alec pried one eye open in a vain attempt to focus on his surroundings. The clock on his dresser indicated the time was seven o'clock in the morning.

"Daddy? Did you forget my birthday?"

What? He bolted upright from the bed, abruptly wide awake. He brought her a present, but had he wrapped it? Had he really forgotten? His mind frantically pinpointed the date. Tuesday. It was Tuesday, July fifteenth.

Shannon collapsed into a fit of giggles, making him realize he'd been had. The little minx. He scrunched his face into a mock frown. "Young lady, your birthday isn't until Saturday. Today is only Tuesday."

"I got you, Daddy. You should have seen your face." She dissolved into another fit of giggles.

"Yeah, you got me," he agreed, a mischievous glint in his eye. "And do you know what that means?"

The giggles abruptly ceased. Shannon gasped in her beautiful brown eyes rounded comically. "What?"

"The Tickle Monster is going to get you." He gave her a fair warning before he pounced. She shrieked, and the sound brought their dog Daisy, a white Westie terrier, galloping to the rescue. Alec kept his touch gentle, but tickled her belly until her giggles filled his head.

There was no better music than the sound of his daughter's laughter.

Daisy, their dog, jumped onto his bed and barked, sticking her nose between them as if trying to figure out how to join the fun as her tail wagged madly.

"Daddy, stop it!" Shannon said between giggles. "You're making Daisy bark."

He nuzzled her neck, paused to press a kiss to her cute little nose and then threw himself back on the bed, his arms outstretched. He grimaced when Daisy licked his face. "He's gone. Daisy scared the Tickle Monster away."

Shannon climbed up to sit on his chest. Her shiny brown hair was tangled from their tussle and he reached up to smooth it back from her face, struck by how Shannon had somehow gotten the best of his and Jenny's genes. "Are you gonna take me and Daisy to the park this morning? You promised."

"Yep." He smiled when she patted his cheek again, apparently fascinated with his bristles. "I think you should probably let me shower and shave first."

She rolled her eyes. "That will take too long. Me and Daisy want to go *now*."

With a chuckle he nodded, unwilling to cause the light to dim from her eyes. Why not? There was plenty of time for him to shave before the start of his shift. "Okay, munchkin. Let's eat something really fast for breakfast and then we'll go to the park."

"I already ate cereal," Shannon said as he padded into the kitchen. He pursed his lips as he surveyed the room. Sure enough, there was an empty bowl surrounded by splashes of milk and other remnants of her breakfast stuck to the table.

Deciding the mess could also wait until later, he grabbed a protein bar to tide him over before changing into a pair of golf shorts and his favorite T-shirt, the one Shannon had bought for his birthday with Andrea's help, that read World's Greatest Dad. Within ten minutes they were on their way outside, Shannon holding Daisy's leash as she skipped beside him.

The park was only a few short blocks from his house, one of the reasons he chosen the property in the first place. The minute he'd found out about Shannon, he hadn't wasted a second in preparing for her to live with him. He'd given up the lease on his bachelor apartment and found a small house in a nice neighborhood in record time. It had needed fixing up, but he worked on the repairs in his spare time. Thankfully, his sister Andrea lived on the opposite side of the park, not too far away for the girls to get together for play dates.

His family had readily supported his decision to become a father for Shannon. He was grateful for their help and unwavering support.

"One of the boys who splashed me hit his head on the bottom of the slide and blood gushed all over!" Shannon repeated the story from her adventure at the water park with relish. He shot her a wry look, wondering when his daughter had developed such a bloodthirsty streak. "Then a grown up put a big white bandage over the bloody part until the ambulance came."

"Really? I hope the cut didn't need stitches." He wondered if the child had been taken to Children's Memorial Hospital, located just a couple blocks from Trinity Medical Center. The thought of Trinity reminded him of Jillian. Shannon continued to chatter about her water park adventure but his attention wandered to the woman who haunted his dreams.

He hadn't been able to call Jillian last night. The hour had gotten so late he hadn't wanted to risk waking her. He glanced at his watch. He could probably call her in a few hours, but he normally reserved his non-work daytime hours for Shannon. The very fact he was tempted to call Jillian anyway irked him. Rafe was the one who needed to interview her. Not him.

He had no business dreaming of Jillian. The way Shannon had woken him that morning patting his cheeks, forced him to remember his priorities.

His daughter was the only woman he needed in his life. At least until she was eighteen and heading off to college. He'd made a silent promise not to cause any upheaval in the little girl's life. She had been through enough, being stuck in foster care for a full month before she'd been allowed to live with him. Besides, he was satisfied with the way things were.

He and Rafe had tracked down the missing boy, Kevin Slutzky, just before midnight. Kevin and his best friend, Steve, had run away, intending to go stay at Steve's father's cabin on Pinecone Lake. They've only gotten as far as Sheboygan, Wisconsin before getting tired and hungry. The story could have ended much worse, and as it was, explaining to Kevin about his mother's heart attack and subsequent hospitalization had been bad enough.

Throughout the search, a small part of him had been very grateful his own little girl had been safely home in bed. He couldn't imagine losing Shannon now that he had her.

A lithe woman was running along the sidewalk circling the park, heading toward them. For a moment he thought he was delusional because her features reminded him of Jillian. As she came closer, he realized the jogger really was Jillian. He smiled and her eyes widened with recognition.

At that moment, Daisy darted into her path.

"Daisy! No!" Shannon tugged sharply on the leash.

Jillian faltered widening per step to avoid the dog, and he reacted instinctively, reaching out for her. He grasped her arm and the momentum caused her to fall against him with enough force to knock his breath away. He took two hasty steps back but managed to hold her upright.

He held her close, for a second or two longer than he should have, enjoying the silky feel of her skin against his and losing himself in the enticing scent of her shampoo. Shannon continued to berate the dog as Jillian grasped his shoulders, shaking one foot to disentangle the leash.

"Sorry about that," he said as she finally freed herself. "Are you alright?"

"Yes, I think so." Her voice was breathless, her face red from exertion. Holding Jillian in his arms was better than anything he could have imagined. He'd wanted to pull her close for a kiss the night he'd walked her to her car at the lakefront, but he hadn't dared touch her, especially in front of Shannon. As if sensing his thoughts, Jillian's eyes widened and lingered on his mouth before she turned to look at Shannon who was crouched beside Daisy. "Hello again, Shannon. How are you?"

"Fine." His daughter's expression was contrite as the dog barked at her feet. "This is my dog, Daisy. She didn't mean to trip you, honest!"

"I know she didn't," Jillian assured her. Reluctantly, Alec allowed her to extricate herself from his embrace so she could reach down to pet Daisy, whose fluffy white body was wiggling with excitement. "She's adorable."

Alec wasn't sure if Jillian was referring to his daughter or dog, but noticed she winced a little when she put her full weight on her foot. He reached for her again, taking her arm. "Easy, I think you've twisted your ankle."

"I'll be fine." Jillian belied her words by reaching down to give her ankle a rub. "I stepped funny, but it wasn't bad."

"There's a park bench just a few feet away." He wrapped a supporting arm around her waist. "Let's have you sit down for a minute."

"I'm fine," she protested, but limped over to the bench. Once they were seated, she wiped her forearm across her brow. "I didn't realize you and Shannon lived around here."

He could have said the same. He hadn't realized Jillian lived so close to him either. And now that he did know, the park might become his favorite place to walk in the mornings. He cleared his throat. "I have a house over on Union Ave."

"My bee sting is all better, see?" Shannon held up her arm.

"Shannon, it's not polite to interrupt," he scolded lightly.

"I do see." Jillian leaned forward, smiling as she examined the bee sting spot on Shannon's arm. "I'm glad you're all better."

"Did you really put stitches in my Daddy?"

Alec frowned, wondering what had made Shelby remember that. After they'd left Jillian on Sunday evening, he'd explained to his daughter how he'd met Jillian at the hospital when she'd taken care of him, although he had been careful not to let the little girl know the wound had been from a knife.

"Yes, I did." Jillian nodded solemnly. "He was very brave, just like you."

Shannon seemed pleased, climbing up on the bench beside her. "Guess what? I'm gonna be a doctor when I grow up, too."

"Really?" Alec and Jillian exclaimed in unison. Jillian laughed and Alec wished he had taken the time to shower and shave before heading out this morning. Then again, if he had, their paths may not have crossed at all.

Better to be scruffy than to miss this.

He turned his attention to his daughter. "No wonder you were so interested in the boy who bled all over the water park."

Jillian raised a brow at his comment. "Hmm. Well, Shannon, if you really want to be a doctor, you have to study really hard in school. Do you like school?" She leaned down to rub her ankle again and Daisy licked her fingers as if to say she was sorry.

"Yes. School is fun," Shannon announced. "I have lots of friends there. They're all coming to my birthday party this Saturday. Will you come, too?"

"Oh, I... uh...I don't know." Jillian's gaze cut to his in a panic.

"That's a great idea," he agreed, ignoring the exasperated look Jillian sent his way. He could tell what she was thinking. She was involved in his case so they shouldn't be spending time together. Yet she wasn't exactly at the top of their list of suspects. Once Rafe finished her interview, there was no reason they couldn't get together as friends at his daughter's party. "There will be at least ten six-year-olds there and I could use all the help I could get." His family planned to chip in to help, but he liked the idea of having Jillian over, too.

"Please?" His daughter turned big, brown, pleading eyes toward Jillian. "That way Daisy will know you're not mad at her."

"I'll stop by if I'm not working," Jillian hedged. "And Daisy already knows I'm not mad at her. Look, she's trying to untie my running shoes."

Shannon giggled when the dog took a shoelace between her teeth and tugged. It was enough to distract his daughter, and she quickly launched into another topic other than her impending birthday party.

Alec knew Jillian had wanted to refuse. Was she really working? Or had it been an excuse?

He should have felt guilty for backing her into a corner, but he didn't. There was nothing wrong with being friends, right? Jillian gave him the impression of being a loner and he'd learned the value of family and friends over this past year.

"I need to get home," Jillian said, breaking into his thoughts.

"We'll walk with you," he said when stood and tested her weight on her ankle.

"There's no need, see?" She lifted her foot and rotated the joint, proving it was uninjured. "I promise it's not painful at all."

"We'll walk you home, anyway," he repeated. The park

was perfectly safe, but if her ankle acted up, he intended to be there for her.

They strolled along the sidewalk surrounding the park. He kept pace with Jillian while Shannon ran ahead with Daisy, running in circles on the grass.

"She's beautiful." This time, he knew she meant Shannon.

"Thanks." His throat closed with pent up emotion. "I feel terrible I wasn't there for her early years, but I cherish every moment I have with her now."

She sent him a sidelong glance. "I know it's not any of my business, but why didn't you know about her?"

It was a fair question. His family had asked the exact same thing. He didn't like admitting his sins, even though he had begged God for forgiveness and was now at peace. "Her mother, Jenny and I were together for about six months but things didn't work out. We were just too different. Honestly, I think part of it was my fault. I wasn't quite ready to settle down, and Jen broke things off."

"But she was pregnant." Jillian frowned.

"She couldn't have known at the time, based on Shannon's birthday. And I certainly didn't know." He couldn't prevent the defensive note in his voice. He didn't like anyone assuming he'd abandoned his responsibilities. "There's no way I would have left if I'd known about Shannon. We shouldn't have gotten ourselves into that situation, anyway. And I take full responsibility for not following up with her afterwards."

"Jenny never contacted you?" She pressed.

He ruefully shook his head. He'd asked himself the same question a dozen times. Why hand Jenny called him? Why hadn't she told him about the baby? He didn't understand, yet she wasn't here to ask. "No, in fact, I'd heard she moved to St. Louis. I'm not sure why she didn't tell me. I feel terrible about that, I'm sure she could have used financial support." It deeply bothered him to think about Jenny carrying the burden of raising a child alone.

"I can imagine," Jillian murmured. Their fingers brushed, clung for a minute, before she pulled away.

He told himself to finish the rest of the story. "It wasn't until ten months ago that I got a call from the Department of Health and Human Services. They contacted me because Jenny had listed me as the father on Shannon's birth certificate. Jen had colon cancer and before she died she gave instructions, requesting Shannon be placed with me." It was the best gift Jenny could have given him.

She raised a brow. "Did you undergo DNA testing? To make sure she's yours?"

"No need." He followed Shannon and Daisy with his gaze as they ran through the park. His tone was firm. "She's mine."

He waited for Jillian to argue—he'd heard it all from his siblings and parents. They'd really wanted him to get a DNA test too. But to his surprise, Jillian didn't push the issue.

"Poor Shannon." She gazed out at his daughter with a frown furrowing in her brow." I imagine how hard it must have been for her, living with a stranger after her mother died."

"It wasn't easy." He paused at the corner of the park, waiting for Shannon and Daisy to catch up. "But we made it. My family helped. A lot." He truly owed his family a debt of gratitude. "Between us, we surround her with love. And as I mentioned, kids are resilient."

"Shannon is blessed to have you. Your family sounds great." Jillian smiled and dropped the subject as Shelby and

Daisy ran back toward them. "This is the road I live on, Fisher Road.

"Fisher Road?" Shannon skipped with Daisy at her heels. "Is that because there are fish nearby?"

"Not that I know of. I'm not sure why they named it that," Jillian admitted.

"Here, take my hand as we cross the street." He reached for Shannon's hand and the three of them and the dog crossed the street. Alec was conscious of how much they probably looked like a typical happy family.

The thought gave him pause. Family was great, but his past experience with relationships had been anything but stellar. The way Jen had disappeared from his life without ever telling him about his daughter was proof of that.

And Shannon needed stability now, more than ever.

"This is it," Jillian said slowing her step.

He was pleased to note her home was similar to his, a cute little Cape Cod. "It's nice."

"Thanks for seeing me home."

"Our pleasure, right, squirt? "He glanced at Shannon.

"Right." His daughter nodded. "Don't forget about my birthday party, Dr. Jillian. Saturday at three."

Alec wished his verbose daughter would shut up about the party already, but Jillian only laughed. "I'll check my schedule."

"That's enough." He gave his daughter a small frown. "Say goodbye."

"Goodbye Dr. Jillian."

"It was nice meeting you again, Shannon." When Jillian glanced at him, he resisted the urge to haul her into his arms to kiss her.

"I'll—uh call you later." He stumbled over the words,

hating the moment of awkwardness. "We—Rafe and I will be in touch. About the interview."

"I understand. I'll be around until three o'clock," Jillian said.

Shannon tugged on his arm impatiently, reminding him that he didn't have free time that afternoon. With regret, he shook his head. "I'm afraid I don't work until this afternoon."

"You're working second shift again, tonight?" Jillian asked.

"Yes, you, too?" He brightened at the prospect.

She nodded. "That's why I said I'm open until three."

"That's when I start, too." Figured their work schedules happened to be one of the few things between them that might match on occasion. "I'll let Rafe know to get in touch with you tonight—if we're not too busy," he cautioned. "If we're slammed with calls, we won't make it." The hard truth was that if he had to respond to violent crimes, interviewing Jillian would fall to the bottom of their list of priorities.

"I understand." Her tone was casual, as if she wouldn't miss him if he couldn't make time for her. She turned to walk up the driveway leading to her house. "Bye, Alec. Bye, Shannon."

"Have a great day." He watched her walk away, wishing desperately that he could follow. He wanted to talk to her some more—and not necessarily about the narcotic case. Despite Shannon tugging on his arm, he didn't move, not an inch, until Jillian had disappeared into her house.

"Come on, Daddy. You said we were going to the park! I didn't get to play on the swing set yet."

"I'm coming." Reluctantly he turned and began walking back the way they'd come.

"I like Dr. Jillian. She's nice."

"Yes, she is." Alec glanced at his daughter, grinning as she jumped and skipped over the cracks in the sidewalk, making a game of their walk. Ruminating over Jillian wasn't smart. Shannon saying Jillian was nice was a far cry from bringing a woman into their lives. That was a complication they didn't need. He didn't have a lot of spare time on his hands or room in his life for relationship, even if the timing was better.

Which it wasn't.

It struck him that a woman like Jillian deserved much more than being relegated to the bottom of his priority list.

CHAPTER SIX

Jillian didn't see Alec that night, or the one after that. Rafe had called her in for an interview, but she'd been disappointed Alec hadn't been anywhere around. The process of being interviewed wasn't as horrible as she'd anticipated. The entire conversation was finished in less than fifteen minutes.

On Thursday she gave herself a stern lecture. It was time to stop acting like an adolescent schoolgirl, waiting for Alec to ask her to the prom. So what if he hadn't made the time to come and see her. The man certainly had his hands full between his career as a police officer and being a single dad.

If only she hadn't run into him at the park. Seeing him in his casual shorts and T-shirt, his cheeks darkened by early morning stubble, grinning with his daughter, had been enough to make her wonder what it would be like to see him like that every day.

The image was so clear she caught her breath. Dreams were one thing, but none of her previous relationships had prepared her for Alec. Every time he was near, she longed for his touch. Even the slightest brush of his fingers against hers had sent a tingle of awareness up her spine. It was difficult to think straight around him.

She gave her head a quick shake. Enough foolishness. All through medical school she'd been focused on her goal of becoming a doctor. Her parents had sacrificed a portion of their retirement fund to finance her education. Graduating at the top of her class had made her mother proud.

Some of her female counterparts had lamented the long hours required of their residency program, claiming their biological clocks were ticking away. She'd never understood the yearning they'd felt, not even when she'd done her obstetrics rotation.

Until now.

She couldn't deny the very tangible connection she felt with Shannon, especially when the girl had leaned against her so trustingly. They had a lot in common. They'd both lost their mothers, and they both cared about Alec.

"Jillian?"

She roused herself from her thoughts and turned to see Dr. Chris Donnell, the chief of staff, approaching. Instinctively she straightened her spine.

"Good evening, Chris. How are you?"

Her boss didn't smile. In fact, his brows were pulled together in a frown. He glanced around and then gently pulled her to a quiet area to talk. Her stomach clenched in warning.

"Do you have any idea who is stealing these narcotics?" His blunt question rocked her back on her heels.

"No. If I did, I'd tell the police."

Chris pursed his lips. "I don't need to tell you, this situation is very disturbing. Anything you can do to find the guilty party and resolve this issue is of utmost importance."

She swallowed hard at his stern tone. At the same time, she lifted her chin. Was he saying this, because he believed she was involved? She prayed that was not the case. "Yes, I completely agree. I've already been interviewed and have changed my password several times. I'm doing my best to keep things under control."

He stared at her for a long moment. "I hope I haven't made a mistake in naming you as the interim medical director, Jillian. I need a true leader in this position."

Her face burned at the implied reprimand but she forced a confidence she didn't quite feel into her tone. "We will find the guilty person. Assigning me this position was not a mistake." She'd learned early on the best way to get ahead in a male dominated profession was to ooze competence while touting your abilities. In other words, act like a guy. "I'm the right person for this role. I'm sure we'll get to the truth very soon."

Her boss gave a brief nod. "I hope you're right. I've had a private meeting with the police on this very issue. They've scheduled an appointment to review how the narcotic dispensing machine works. Please go and offer your assistance."

"Of course." It took a second for his statement to register. Alec was here? She glanced around the arena, and then spotted him standing off to one side next to Rafe. She crossed over, greeting them both, but a warm glow burned in her belly when Alec's gaze lingered on hers in a special, silent greeting.

"I thought you guys had already gotten a demonstration on this machine," Jillian said.

"No, unfortunately things have been crazy." Alec waved a hand. "Would you mind showing us how this works?"

Step by step she went through the mechanics of the dispensing machine noting the numbness and tingling in her fingers, curiously absent over the past few days, had returned. She kept up her routine of running three miles every other morning and so far she hadn't noticed anything different. The five percent chance of having multiple sclerosis or some other auto-immune disorder seemed more and more distant.

But that was just foolish, wishful thinking.

"Dr. Davis, there's a victim of a motor vehicle crash coming in," Lacy informed her once she'd finished the demonstration.

She glanced down at her phone with a frown. "Oh? Why didn't we get a trauma call?"

At that moment the pager app on her phone dinged. She raised a brow.

"Yeah, we're having some trouble with our paging system," Lacy admitted. "Don't worry, someone's here from IT, looking into it."

"Good to know. Thanks." She read the message on her display. Fifty-two-year-old white male being admitted with blunt trauma to the chest and head from an airbag deployment secondary to a car crash. Vitals stable. It didn't sound too bad, for a trauma call.

"We're putting him in trauma bay one." Lacy gestured to the large electronic board where a man's name had just been populated into the assigned slot. "If he's stable, we can always move him into a different room."

"Great. If you need anything else in the meantime, let me know." She glanced back toward Rafe and Alec. "I'm sorry, I need to get back to work. Is there anything else you need?"

"Just a quick question." Alec frowned. "I noticed you

used a password to get into the machine. I assume you changed it recently based on the meeting we had the other day. But I could see what you entered while standing behind you."

She flushed. "Yes, it's not the most foolproof system in the world. I confess, I didn't try to hide my password from you as I didn't think it was necessary. Typically, I do better. And we have recommended that all staff change their passwords every week for the interim. Or more often if they think someone else may have seen it."

"I understand." He and Rafe exchanged a glance. Alec continued, "Do you think they're really going to cooperate by changing their password each week?"

She grimaced. "I don't know. I would like to think so, but you know how it is. We need passwords for everything. Making up new ones and keeping track of them is a pain in the behind."

"Yeah." He nodded thoughtfully. "I think we'll hang around for a while, if you don't mind."

She shrugged. "Suit yourself."

Within minutes she heard the doors to the ambulance bay open, announcing the arrival of their blunt force trauma patient. She hurried over to the first bed in the trauma bay.

"Vital signs are good, although his blood pressure is on the high side, not sure what his baseline is," the paramedic announced. "Glasgow Coma Score of 20, responding to verbal commands. He has an eighteen-gauge left peripheral IV placed in the field, 500 cc's of normal saline infused."

William Patterson, one of the emergency department nurses working in the trauma room connected the patient to the heart monitor.

She remembered seeing his name on the electronic board as Barry Cox. She approached his bedside, leaning over the gurney to examine him. Barry was an extremely large man with a bloody gash across his forehead. A strong odor of alcohol emanated from him, which she tried to ignore as she assessed his neural status for herself. "Mr. Cox? Can you open your eyes for me?"

Her patient opened his eyes, saw her leaning close and suddenly went wild. She reared backward when he bolted upright on the gurney, the abrupt movement yanking the IV out of his left arm. Barry grabbed the heart electrodes William had connected, yanking hard and dropping them on the floor.

"I'll get you for this!" Barry shouted, swinging his arm toward Jillian with the intention of hitting her. "I'll get you!"

She tried to duck away from the blow, but his fist connected with her right shoulder, causing a sharp pain to zing down her arm. Before she realized what was happening, Alec was there, placing himself between her and the wild patient.

"Mr. Cox, you better calm down." Alex's tone was even although his eyes flashed with a glint of anger. William, the paramedics and Alec tried to surround the patient, but they couldn't get too close. He was still waving his arms in a threatening manner. "The staff here want to help you, but not if you're going to fight against them."

"I don't need any help!" Barry jumped out of gurney and stood swaying on his feet. Jillian suspected his head and chest, both which had been hit by the airbag from the steering wheel, hurt like the dickens. Or maybe he didn't feel any pain through his alcohol haze. "Leave me alone!"

She tried to step around Alec, but he frowned and moved so his body remained between her and Barry. She stifled a sigh and captured Barry's gaze, imploring him to listen. "Mr. Cox, please, sit down. I need to make sure you don't have a head injury or any cracked ribs. Does your chest hurt?"

As if on cue, Barry rubbed the center of his chest. "Yeah, it hurts a little."

She managed to edge around Alec, whose gaze was trained on their patient. "My name is Dr. Davis. I'd really like to examine you. What if you have other injuries?"

"I'm fine." He took a step backward and Alec followed. Barry frantically searched for the door. "I just want to go home."

Boy, he was stubborn. "Mr. Cox, you can't go home until I examine you."

"I can go home if I say I'm going home." Barry took another step in the general direction of the ambulance bay doors. "You can't stop me. I have rights."

"You do have rights, but I think we need to make sure you don't have a head injury that might be clouding your judgment." As much as she wanted to let Barry walk out the door, she was medically liable for his care. She could not let him go until she saw the CT scan of his brain. If the scan was negative, she'd be more than happy to discharge him. "Why don't you just cooperate with us? Once we make sure you don't have a head injury, I'll discharge you home."

For a moment she thought she had him, but he turned and bolted to the door. Before anyone could move to follow, he stumbled and fell, his head bouncing off the linoleum floor.

Alec and the paramedics went over and secured his arms and legs so he couldn't hurt himself or others.

"Give him 5 milligrams of Haldol intramuscularly so we can get his IV replaced," Jillian ordered. William dashed over to get the medication.

Barry struggled, babbling nonsense as Alec and the

paramedics held him down. Once William had given the sedative, Jillian came up to kneel beside Alec. "Whenever you're ready, we'll lift him back up onto the gurney."

"We'll lift him—just get out of the way."

Startled by Alex's abrupt tone, she backed off and the three men lifted the heavy patient back onto the gurney. They continued to hold Barry's extremities while she placed another IV.

When Barry began to struggle again, she shook her head. "I may have to intubate him so that we can give him major sedation to get the CT scan of his head. I'm really worried he has a head injury, especially since he's not making much sense anymore."

"Here's the airway box." William set the intubation supplies on her right.

She could feel Alec's gaze on her as she prepared to intubate their patient. Holding the laryngoscope and her right hand wasn't easy and she prayed her fingers wouldn't go numb as she lifted Barry's jaw enough to visualize the airway. Just as she slid the endotracheal tube into his larynx, the laryngoscope slipped. She bit her lip as she advanced the tube blindly, praying she'd inserted it in the correct place. "I need the respiratory therapist to assist with checking tube placement."

A respiratory therapist whose name tag read Michelle stepped forward placing a small device on the end of the endotracheal tube. "Placement looks good, Dr. Davis."

Jillian nodded and reached for her stethoscope. "Michelle, please hold this tube secure. I still want to listen." When she heard breath sounds in both lungs, overwhelming relief made her knees weak. Her numbness and tingling hadn't hurt the patient, thankfully. She nodded at William. "It's in. Give him five milligrams of Versed." Then she turned to Michelle. "Please connect him to the ventilator." She went on to reiterate what ventilator settings she wanted, then stepped back.

After the medication was administered every muscle in Barry Cox's body relaxed. Alec and the paramedics were finally able to let go.

"Thank you everyone." She glanced around to find the nurse. "William please call radiology, let them know we need a stat CT of the head. I'll enter the order."

"Will do." William grabbed the nearest phone. It didn't take long for her to enter the order into the computer. A few minutes later, William said, "Good news, they're ready for him now."

"Great." She stepped back. "I hope he sleeps like a baby the entire time."

"Me, too," William commented in a dry tone as he and Michelle coordinated pushing the gurney while giving breaths via an Ambu bag. They quickly wheeled Barry away.

She lifted a hand to rub the spot where Barry's fit had connected with her shoulder.

"Are you okay?" Alec looked concerned. "Why on earth didn't you get out of the way?"

She gave him an exasperated look. "I'm fine. This sort of thing is not uncommon. I'll get some ibuprofen. Thanks for all your help, please excuse me." She turned and head back to her office. She needed a moment alone and besides, there was a stash of ibuprofen somewhere in her desk, she was certain.

Alec followed. "Maybe you should call one of the orthopedic surgeons to take a look at your arm."

Ignoring him, she found the ibuprofen and dropped three tablets into the palm of her hand. Her fingers still held a slight tremor from the near assault. Or maybe it was her undiagnosed Multiple Sclerosis. She tossed them back with some water from a half finished water bottle on her desk. The physical altercation with Barry Cox had unsettled her more than she wanted to admit. "It's just a minor muscle ache, he didn't hit me very hard."

Alec scowled. "Looked hard enough from where I was standing. And I noticed your hand was affected—you almost dropped the laryngoscope. I'm worried about you."

The close call with the laryngoscope had been too much. What if she'd harmed the patient? She flexed her fingers and abruptly sat down behind her desk. After the emotionally draining situation, she didn't have the energy to lie. Better he knew the truth anyway. "The problem with my hand isn't related to my shoulder."

Alec crossed over, pushed a pile of paperwork aside so he could sit on the corner of her desk, facing her. "What is the problem, then?"

He was close, too close, and the need to seek refuge in his arms was strong. Tears burned her eyes but she quickly blinked them away. "I honestly don't know. My neurologist can't seem to find a diagnosis. But it might be serious."

"Neurologist?" Alec reached over and took one of her hands in his. "Has he ordered testing?"

His hand felt so warm and strong around hers. She stared at their entwined fingers for a moment. Then took a deep breath and nodded. "Next Tuesday I'm having evoked potentials done." At his confused expression she went on to explain, "It's a test where they poke needles into my nerves in order to measure the response."

"Ouch," he muttered. He drew her up to her feet, urging her close. "I'm so sorry. If there's anything I can do..."

"There isn't." But it was sweet of him to ask. He

continued to pull her closer until she was wrapped in his arms in a secure hug. Giving in to the need to be held, she briefly rested her head on his shoulder. She allowed herself a moment of absorbing his strength. He stroked a hand down her back and she wished she could stay like that for the rest of the night. But she couldn't. In fact, another patient could come in at any second.

With regret Jillian lifted her head and glanced up at Alec, intending to thank him. Before she could form the words, he dipped his head and captured her mouth with his.

He tasted like cinnamon and coffee. She parted her lips, inviting more. He didn't hesitate to deepen their kiss. Seconds extended into long minutes as the kiss changed from something sweet to something edgy.

In some just some part of her brain she knew he meant to offer comfort, but there was nothing simple about the way their mouths fused as one. She'd never been impacted like this by a simple kiss. There was absolutely nothing simple about it.

Her pager app went off with a shrill beep. She wished she could ignore it, but obviously couldn't. Breaking away from Alec, breathing heavily, she groped for her phone. With an effort, she focused her gaze on the words on the screen.

"They must have fixed the paging system. I have another patient coming in." Her voice sounded husky to her own ears. "A woman with belly pain."

"How long until she shows up?" His voice was low, gravely.

"Any minute now." She stepped back, not that there was a whole lot of room between her desk and the wall. "I really have to go."

He nodded, running his hand through his dark hair.

The frustration on his features made her want to smile. "Do you work on Saturday?"

"No." At first she thought he was going to ask her out, then belatedly remembered his daughter's party. "Alec, I don't think—"

"Shannon's been asking about you," he interrupted. "You're her hero after the bee sting. She keeps talking about wanting to be a doctor, just like you. Would you please come, even for a short time? It would mean a lot to her."

And to him? The unspoken question hovered there between them. She knew going to his house, to his daughter's birthday party, was treading on dangerous ground. But right now, with her lips tingling from his kiss, and his intoxicating scent swirling through her brain, she couldn't refuse. Especially because she couldn't bring herself to disappoint Shannon. She managed a nod. "I'd love to come. Three o'clock, right?"

His lips curved in a grin. "Right." He turned and plucked a pen from her desk and scribbled his address and phone number on a scrap of paper. "Call me if something comes up and you can't make it. I'll explain to Shannon that your ability to attend depends on work. She'll understand."

Clearly, Alec would do anything to protect his daughter, even if that meant making up an excuse on her behalf. Rather than being annoyed by the knowledge, she was touched by his concern. Did he really expect her to renege on the party? She had her doubts about going, but she wouldn't deliberately lie to him. Or to his daughter.

"Nothing will keep me away from Shannon's party, short of a busload of trauma patients." She lightly touched his arm. "I promise."

She didn't make promises likely. The way he held her gaze convinced her he understood. He took her hand and brushed a quick kiss along her knuckles. She caught her breath, taken aback by the sweet, gallant gesture.

"Thank you. I can't wait to see you again."

His words sent a shaft of longing radiating down her spine. "Me, too," she whispered.

CHAPTER SEVEN

Alec found himself anxiously waiting, with about as much patience as Shannon, for the hour of her party to arrive.

For one thing, he'd be relieved when his job of hosting ten six-year-olds was over. He wanted everything to go off without a hitch for his daughter's sake. Shannon deserved a memorable celebration for her sixth birthday. Her first without her mother.

But he couldn't lie to himself. The main reason he was looking forward to today was because he desperately wanted to see Jillian again.

Kissing her had rocked him back on his heels. He'd been unable to erase the taste of her from his mind. And frankly, he wanted to kiss her again. Soon. During the brief interlude in her office, he'd completely forgotten where they were. Until her pager had gone off.

He hadn't dated anyone since taking custody of Shannon. He'd been single-minded in his goal to create a loving home for his daughter. Yet one electrifying kiss had reminded him of everything he was missing.

And then there was that promise he'd made not to

create any upheaval in Shannon's life.

Why did that promise seem so foolish now?

He shook his head. If he had half a brain, he'd call Jillian and let her off the hook as far as attending Shannon's party. His daughter likely wouldn't notice her absence. He felt certain that once Shannon was surrounded by her friends, thoughts of grown-ups would vanish from her mind.

His daughter had to be his primary concern. She had been through the most difficult transition he could imagine, losing her mother to cancer and then moving miles away to live with a father she didn't know. Not to mention the month she'd stayed in a foster home. Upsetting the peaceful balance they'd found over the past few months was not an option.

Which meant no more kissing Jillian. He repeated that to himself for extra emphasis. They would only be friends. That would be the best way to handle things moving forward. In her office, she'd seem so lonely. No one should have to imagine taking a painful test where they stuck needles into your nerves, all alone.

He wished he could talk to her about the narcotic case, but that subject was off limits. He and Rafe had interviewed the staff members along with a handful of kids on the Barclay Park football team, but no one gave them much of anything to go on. He'd hoped members of the football team would provide info, but every kid denied having seen Ricky, the boy who'd been killed, with any drugs in his possession.

Rafe thought they should concentrate on the hospital staff, not the football players. Yet he couldn't help thinking the two were related. He'd played football in high school and the morning after a tough game his entire body had hurt. Maybe it was a stretch, but it was the only theory he could come up with. He was determined to find a connection between the Barclay Park football team and someone within the emergency department of Trinity Medical Center.

Daisy barked like a mad dog, diverting his attention to the upcoming party. Shannon ran into the kitchen to get him.

"Daddy! The giant blow up games are here!"

"I'm coming." Setting his coffee aside, he allowed his daughter to drag him outside. Sure enough, the inflatable slide and mini trampoline were being assembled in his backyard.

Shannon hopped from one foot to the other, radiating excitement. "Can I try them out before my friends get here? Please?"

"Sweetheart, it's going to take these guys at least an hour to get them inflated. Come inside for now and we'll test your games later."

Dejected, Shannon took Daisy back inside the house. Alec spent a few minutes making sure the team setting up the play equipment had everything they needed before he went back inside.

In the kitchen, he finished his coffee, and then went through his mental checklist. Pizza? Check. Cake? Check. Ice cream? Check. Goodie bags? Check. Balloons? Check. What on earth was he forgetting? Oh yeah, juice boxes. Check.

Who knew having a birthday party was so much work? He took a deep breath. Everything was ready to go. All he needed was to shower and change. In less than an hour, his family would descend upon him.

And despite his internal let's-be-friends speech, he was more than a little curious to see how well Jillian got along with his family.

HIS FAMILY WAS EARLY. Bless their hearts, his sisters Andrea and Amber were worried he wouldn't have things under control.

For once he showed them he was capable of being a good father. Or at least a responsible one.

He didn't mind when they helped him clean up the house, even though he knew the place would be trashed by the time Shannon's friends left. His family's efforts to support him since he'd taken custody of Shannon were very much appreciated.

One by one Shannon's guests arrived. Each of the parents promised to return in four hours, at seven o'clock that evening to pick up their little darlings. As several of the girls shrieked and ran around, making Daisy bark, Alec silently prayed he would last that long.

Once all the girls were present and accounted for, Alec and his brother Adam supervised the kids as they played on the inflatable slide and trampoline. He didn't even notice when Jillian arrived until Andrea came out to replace him.

"Better go and chat with your friend." Andrea nodded in Jillian's direction. "She looks a little shell shocked over there. It's almost as if she'd never been to a kid's party before."

"Thanks." He didn't need to be told twice. As he approached, he heard Amber giving Jillian a brief history on every member of the entire Monroe family.

"Adam is a pediatrician, you'll have a lot in common with him. Andrea used to be a nurse, but she quit her job after she had Beth because her husband Stuart travels too much for her to have a set schedule. Austin is a firefighter and just left to head back to California. Aaron is a heart surgeon in Boston." Amber flashed Alec a wide, cheeky grin when she saw him. "Hey, Alec. I'm helping Jillian put names to faces.

"Thanks Amber, but I think you've overwhelmed her." He noticed Jillian clutched a large gift wrapped box, her eyes wide as she took in the adults scattered among the girls. "Hey, don't worry," he quickly assured her." You already meant Adam, right? Austin isn't here and neither is Aaron, so those are two less family members to worry about. I promise there's no test on everyone's names."

"To think I used to ace tests." Jillian shook her head and offered a faint smile. "Hi." She thrust the box into his hands. "This is for Shannon."

"Great. I'm sure she'll love it. Come in, I have a few soft drinks to offer, you won't be forced to pick from the selection of juice boxes."

They headed into the house, Amber following hot on their heels. Jillian glanced around, seemingly curious to see how he lived. He silently thanked his sisters for their cleaning efforts.

"So, Jillian, how long have you known my brother?" Amber didn't seem to realize she was being incredibly nosy. Or rather, she didn't care. He used to butt into her personal life, too, but that had stopped after her marriage to Nick. Enough with the payback already, he thought wryly.

"A few months," Jillian admitted. "I stitched up his knife wound when he came into the emergency department."

He hid a wince as he placed Jillian's gift amongst the others in one corner of the living room.

"Knife wound?" Amber swung around to pin him with a narrow gaze. "And why didn't I hear anything about a knife wound?"

"Why do you think?" Ignoring his younger sister, he turned to Jillian. "What would you like to drink? Coffee? Water? Soda?"

"I think I'll stick with water for now." He frowned a little because Jillian definitely looked uncomfortable.

"Relax, I swear my family is harmless." He guided her to the kitchen to hand her a bottle of water. "They talk a lot, but just ignore them."

"Maybe, but I didn't realize there'd be so many of them."

He sighed. "I know. All of our names starting with the letter A doesn't help." He lifted a hand. "And don't say it, we've heard all the A-Team jokes known to man."

She laughed and he relaxed, escorting her back outside to meet his parents. He made the introductions but there wasn't time for more questions because Shannon ran over when she caught sight of Jillian.

"Dr. Jillian!" Shannon threw her arms around Jillian's waist for a quick hug. "Thanks for coming to my party."

"Thank you for inviting me." Jillian returned Shannon's hug and Alec was struck by how natural they looked together. Jillian glanced over to where the kids were taking turns going down the inflatable slide. "Looks like you're having fun."

"Lots of fun. My dad is the best dad in the whole world!" Shannon broke away from Jillian to treat him to an exuberant hug before running back to join her friends.

"You heard her," Alec said jokingly. "If anyone needs me, I'll be out buying a pony." He couldn't help the goofy grin that spread across his features.

"Don't let Shannon hear you say that," Andrea said with a chuckle. "She might hold you to it."

Alec half expected Jillian to take off after the first hour, but she hung in there through games, pizza, cake and ice cream and finally the gift opening. When Shannon sat down to open her presents, she reached for Jillian's first.

"A doctor's bag!" Alex's jaw dropped when Shannon opened a doctor's kit. Only this one was nothing like the plastic ones you got in the stores. Jillian had put together a real bag full of actual instruments and supplies—all child friendly of course. "I love it, Dr. Jillian. Thanks so much!"

"You are very welcome." Jillian blushed as almost every Monroe stared at her, as if gauging how close she was to becoming a permanent member of the family.

He tried not to sigh. His family meant well, but Jillian wasn't in the running to become Shannon's stepmother.

Was she?

No. That was not an option. She was simply a generous person. He knew the only reason Jillian had come to the party at all was because she hadn't wanted to disappoint Shannon. And he was grateful for that.

Turning his attention back to his daughter, he watched as she went through the rest of her presents. There was still time to play after the gift opening before parents returned to pick up their children, so he shooed the girls back outside. Shannon carefully carried her precious gifts into her bedroom.

He quickly followed the dozen girls to keep an eye on them. Heaven forbid anything happened to one of them while under his care. He stood by the inflatable slide, waiting for Shannon to return. When she didn't come back outside right away, he left Adam in charge and headed back into the house.

Walking down the hall towards Shannon's room, he heard voices. Slowing his steps, he shamelessly eavesdropped.

"My mommy died of cancer," Shannon was saying in a matter-of-fact tone. "And the doctors tried to save her life, but they couldn't. I think by the time I'm a grown up, doctors will know how to cure cancer, don't you?"

"Yes, I do." Jillian's voice was soft. "I think you're a very brave girl to want to help others."

"When I first came here to live, I cried a lot because I missed my mommy," Shannon said in a low voice. "But now I have my daddy, and my grandma and my grandpa, and my aunts and uncles. Oh, and my cousins Beth and Ben. A whole family of my own."

"You have a wonderful family," Jillian murmured.

"Yes, I know. Especially my Daddy. I love him best of all. Do you like my Daddy, Dr. Jillian?"

There was a long pause and Alec held his breath waiting for Jillian's answer.

"Of course I like your Daddy. He's a very nice man."

"Good. Because I think he likes you, too."

Whoa, what is this? His six-year-old daughter was arranging his love life? Deciding he'd eavesdropped long enough, he wrapped on the door frame a moment before entering Shannon's room. Both Shannon and Jillian were sitting cross legged on the floor, the real doctor's bag between them.

"There you are. Your friends are all outside, Shannon. You should go out and say your goodbyes because their parents will be coming to pick them up soon."

"Okay, Daddy." Shannon jumped to her feet. He crossed over to offer Jillian a hand to help her up. "Thanks again for coming to my party." Shannon gave Jillian another quick hug before dashing outside to join her friends.

"What was that all about?" He felt guilty for asking as he'd already overheard a good portion of their conversation.

Jillian's gaze was serious. "Nothing really. A little girl talk, that's all."

He told himself now to push for more. He was glad Jillian was there for his daughter. He reached up to tuck a strand of Jillian's hair behind her ear. "I want you to know how much I appreciate you coming today. Your presence meant a lot to Shannon." After a moment's hesitation, he added, "And to me. Honestly, you have no idea how terrifying ten young girls can be."

She laughed. "If you think they're terrifying now, wait until they're sixteen and getting ready to go to the prom."

The image of Shannon wearing an evening dress with her hair piled on her head made him wince. He put a hand to his chest and pressed against his sternum. "Don't. Please. I can't go there yet."

Her smile was surprisingly sad. "I think you're going to do just fine."

She moved to step past him, intent on leaving Shannon's room, but he caught her hand in his. "What's wrong?"

"Nothing." Was it his imagination or was her bright smile a bit forced? "Come on, you'd head out there to say goodbye to your daughter's guests too. Their parents will expect you to be there."

She was right, so he reluctantly dropped the subject. The parents showed up on time, thank goodness, but he was more than a little disappointed to discover Jillian slipped away during the chaos.

Without saying goodbye.

GUILT PLAGUED JILLIAN the rest of the weekend. Coward, she admonished herself for the tenth time. She'd taken advantage of the confusion of departing partygoers to leave without speaking to Alec again.

She'd been too afraid he'd notice how hard she was trying not to cry.

Shannon was an amazing little girl. Very bright. Perceptive. Older than her years, mostly due, Jillian suspected, to dealing with her mother's illness. Her heart had ached when the little girl had confessed her dream of becoming a doctor because she wanted to be like the doctors who had taken care of her mother.

And Shannon's hero worship of her father was understandable as well. Clearly, Alec was as devoted to her as Shannon was to him. Most of all Jillian had been touched at the way Shannon had included her in her generous hugs.

Tears pricked her eyes and she blinked them back with an effort. Since when had she become so emotional? Listening as Shannon had talked about her mother's death, she had remembered her own mother's pain filled demise from multiple sclerosis. Granted, Jillian had been an adult when her mother passed away, not a young child, but sharing that moment with Shannon had made her face a harsh truth.

Until she knew what was wrong with her, she had no business getting close to Alec and Shannon. The last thing Shannon needed was to live through another loss.

She took a deep breath and let it out slowly. Enough wallowing in self-pity. So what if she'd enjoyed the lively chaos created by the Monroe family? She should be happy to have spent a nice day with them, instead of ruminating in the uncertainty of her illness. As an only child of older parents, she'd never been exposed to the incessant teasing the Monroe's had subjected each other too. She'd been secretly thrilled at how they'd included her in the mix.

"Hey, Jillian, did my brother cry like a baby when you stitched up his wound?" Andrea had asked. "He certainly bawled hard enough when he fell off his bike when he was eight."

"Speaking of a baby, we had some interesting pictures of Alec as a baby. Mom? Do you have Alec's baby pictures handy?" Amber had added in a teasing tone. "I bet Jillian would love to see them."

Alec had taken their teasing in stride, and even Amber had commented on it. "Alec, I can't believe how laid back you are. What happened to the uptight guy I used to know? The one who practically stalked me when I was dating Nick? Are you trying to impress Jillian or what?"

He'd simply grinned and shrugged, refusing to rise to the bait. Jillian could tell they were close, although she got the impression Alec hadn't always been as included in family gatherings as he was now.

Members of the Monroe family had given her a couple of curious stares but overall they'd accepted her presence at Shannon's party without question. She'd never felt so welcomed by a large family.

At some point during the rest of the weekend she half expected Alec to call, bringing her rude behavior to the forefront. But he didn't. Her stomach went queasy when she realized he might be angry with her.

And suddenly the thought of never speaking to Alec again was unbearable. With determination she pulled out her phone along with the small scrap of paper he'd given her with his number on it and dialed. Relief warred with disappointment when the call went to voicemail.

"Alec, I'm sorry I left so quickly yesterday. Please forgive me. I had a wonderful time." She hesitated, tempted to add more, but forced herself to press the end button.

Hopefully he would accept her apology. And maybe he would even contact her.

But as the hours ticked away, Alec didn't return her call.

TUESDAY MORNING JILLIAN dragged herself out of bed, scrubbing the grit from her eyes. Another restless night. She'd been anxious about her upcoming evoked potential testing, tossing and turning, trying to pray for peace, even as her mind darted back to the upcoming appointment. She was afraid of the test itself, almost as much as what the results might be.

She'd worked a day shift on Monday, and thankfully things had been relatively quiet. No major trauma victims, although the steady stream of patients had kept her busy enough to make the time pass quickly. No missing narcotics, either which had also been a relief.

Annoyingly enough, she'd spent most of the time expecting Alec to drop by. By the time she'd gone home, she'd reminded herself that getting involved with Alec and Shannon was a bad idea.

Hadn't she decided not to have expectations for her future until she knew what was wrong with her? Yes. And apparently, Alec felt the same way.

After crawling from bed and taking a quick shower, she dressed in a pair of shorts and a baggy t-shirt as she'd been told to wear loose clothing.

She decided to skip breakfast. The instructions for the test limited her to clear liquids which meant she couldn't even have coffee as she preferred a heavy dose of cream. Fearing she might throw up anyway, it was probably better to go without. On her way to the hospital, her stomach gurgled as if it was full of jumping beans fighting for a way out.

The evoked potential testing was done in the neurology clinic. She made her way to the third floor and after checking in, took a seat in the waiting room. It felt odd to be on the other side of the clinic setting, as a patient instead of being the physician in charge.

After ten long agonizing minutes, she debated going back up to the desk to remind the staff she was still waiting. Didn't they know how long ten minutes was when you were sitting around, doing nothing, and expecting the worst?

"Jillian?"

She heard her name, not from the staff seated behind the clinic desk but from somewhere behind her. She swiveled in her seat. Surprised, she gaped at Alec's tall, broad shouldered frame. He was casually dressed in jeans and polo shirt, a serious expression carved into his features.

"Shannon?" She shot to her feet, imagining there could only be one reason for Alec to be in the hospital on his day off. "What happened to Shannon?"

He tilted his head, giving her a puzzled look. "Shannon is fine. She's spending the morning with Andrea's kids Bethany and Benjamin."

Shannon was fine. Not a patient at Children's Memorial Hospital. Alec's daughter was fine. She let out her breath in a whoosh.

"Good. I'm glad." She frowned. I don't understand. What are you doing here? "

Alec stepped forward, took her arm and gently eased back into her seat. He met her gaze steadily. "I came here to be with you. I saw the test information on your desk the other day. You mentioned this was a painful procedure and I didn't want you to face it alone."

CHAPTER EIGHT

Jillian stared at Alec in dazed wonder. He'd purposefully glanced at the note on her desk, memorizing the date and time of her testing. He had come in on his precious time off work just to be with her.

Ridiculous tears threatened once again, burning the backs of her eyelids. A lump formed in her throat, making speech impossible.

"I'm sorry I didn't have time to talk to you Sunday or Monday," Alec continued. "I took time off work to spend a few days with Shannon." He wrinkled his nose. "Andrea and I took the girls on a train ride to Chicago, to visit a large doll store. We stayed the night in a hotel then came home the next day." He grinned. "You'll be glad to know that next to her new doll, Shannon has claimed your doctor's bag as her favorite gift."

"I'm glad." She managed to force the words past her constricted throat. "Sounds like you had a great time."

Alec relaxed back in his seat, his expression wry. "I can't say the doll store was at the top of my list of places to visit, but it was worth the trip to see the excitement in Shannon's eyes. She and Bethany were in doll heaven."

"I'm sure she was thrilled." Alec was a good father to Shannon. First he'd taken her to the children's tent at the festival of arts, had a birthday party at his house and then topped the little girl's birthday weekend off with a trip to Chicago. Imagining him knee deep in a myriad of dolls and frilly clothes made her smile. She loved her father, but she'd lost him too young. She missed him. Missed the closeness Shannon shared with Alec.

"Jillian Davis?" A woman wearing scrubs stood in the doorway of the clinic, looking at her expectantly.

"Yes. I'm here." She stood, disconcerted when Alec rose to his feet, too. Clearly he'd been serious about accompanying her. She flushed. "Don't feel is if you need to come in with me." She was a bit embarrassed that she'd been such a chicken about this test. "I'm sure I'll be fine."

"Don't argue. I'm coming in with you, and that's that." His chin was set at a stubborn angle that reminded her of Shannon.

"Okay." She gave up trying to fight him, especially since her nerves were on edge. Squaring her shoulders, she stepped forward walking past the front desk toward the woman standing in the hallway. She reminded herself that the shocks were only a little painful, but that didn't really ease her anxiety. Having Alec close at hand would certainly serve as a distraction.

The clinic nurse led them to a room at the end of a long hallway. Inside there was an exam table, two hard plastic chairs, and a large machine. She knew about evoked potentials but had not witnessed one being done during her medical training. It was a diagnostic test that was never performed in the emergency department.

"Please have a seat." The nurse smiled as if to assure her the test would be all over in a jiffy.

Jillian reluctantly sat on the exam table. "Do I need to wear a gown?"

"No, you're wearing shorts and a T-shirt. That should be fine."

Jillian nodded in relief.

"Dr. Juran will be here in a minute to explain the details of both a visual and sensory evoked potential testing. After that, I'll be back to start the procedure."

"Thank you," Jillian murmured.

When the nurse left them alone in the room Alec reached for her hand, his long fingers engulfing hers. "Nervous?"

She lifted a shoulder. "Yes, a little." She stared at their clasped hands, unable to convince herself to let go.

"Don't worry." His voice was low and reassuring. "I'll be with you the entire time."

She was touched by his kindness.

Within moments Dr. Juran knocked on the door and came in. "Jillian, how are you?"

She tugged her fingers from Alec's so she could shake his hand. "I'm fine." When she noted his gaze darted curiously to Alec, she introduced them. "This is a friend of mine, Alec Monroe. Alec, Dr. Juran, Chief of Neurology here at Trinity Medical Center."

"Monroe." Dr. Juran gave Alec a quizzical look. "There's a pediatrician on staff at Children's Memorial whose last name is Monroe. He recently referred an adolescent patient to me."

Alec nodded. "Adam is my older brother."

"He's a good doctor." Dr. Juran sat down and turned to Jillian. "I'm planning to do both visual and sensory evoked potential testing today. The procedures have very little risk and will probably take about ninety minutes to complete."

"Why do the sensory testing?" She asked. "I read how multiple sclerosis is diagnosed by visual testing,"

"Ah, but we don't have a diagnosis of multiple sclerosis yet, do we?" Dr. Juran smiled. "I need to do comprehensive testing if I'm to figure out what is wrong with you. Please trust me to be the neurology expert, hmm?"

She flushed, knowing he was right. She hunched her shoulders. "I will, but that doesn't mean I'm going to stop asking questions."

"I'd be disappointed if you did," he assured her. "Cora will attach the electrodes to your scalp. The visual testing will be first, and then we'll do the sensory testing." He must have noticed her expression because he patted her knee as if she were a small child instead of a thirty-one-year-old woman. And a colleague. "The sensory testing won't take too long, I promise. I'll be as quick as possible."

She didn't doubt him. In fact, she'd researched the neurologists with the best reputation before deciding to approach Dr. Juran. "I know."

Alec didn't say much, but his presence beside her was more comforting than she'd anticipated. As soon as the electrodes had been attached to her scalp, he'd taken her hand firmly in his and she sensed this time he wasn't going to let go.

The visual testing took longer than she thought it would. But then Cora informed her they were now switching to the sensory testing. Instinctively, she tightened her grip on Alec's hand.

"Can you give her something for pain?" He asked.

"I'm afraid not," Cora responded. "Narcotics would

mess up the results. But we'll try to be quick. We'll start with your feet and calves."

The first electrical shock made her suck in a harsh breath. It wasn't as bad as she'd been expecting, but not comfortable either. She was more prepared for the next shock but the higher on her extremities they went, the more the shocks hurt. One painful jolt piled on top of another, increasing her sensitivity to them. When they're finished with both of her legs, Cora moved to her arms, forcing Alec to let go of her hand.

"Talk to me," Jillian begged, gritting her teeth as she endured one electrical shock after the other. "Tell me about yourself."

Alec seemed to know exactly what she needed. "You already know I come from a big family. I used to be known as the wild child. School didn't come easy for me, so I graduated from high school with dismal grades. I didn't have many college options, so I joined the army. Considering how several members of my family were in the medical profession, I requested to be trained as a medic."

She concentrated on his words and on not yelping in pain when the electrical shock zapped a nerve she hit didn't even know she had.

"Being a medic in the army is much like your job in the emergency department—you never know what injuries you'll see. After a while, though, my superiors noticed I possessed other skills that were generally more useful."

"Like what?" She looked at him, concentrating on the deep, rich timber of his voice.

"My sharp shooting skills." For a moment a dark shadow flashed over his eyes. Then she wondered if she'd imagined it, because it was gone. "They were impressed I always hit my target dead center, no matter what distance I was shooting from. So they moved me out of the medical program."

"How long were you in the army?"

"One six-week tour. After leaving the army I decided to go into law enforcement. The rest is history."

And that was too bad. She thought he would have had a great career in the medical field. "Why were you known as the wild Monroe?" She asked, both to keep him talking and because she really wanted to know.

"I always managed to get into trouble. More than anyone else in my family. My friend Timmy and I were known for doing wacky things. One day we caught four bumblebees in a coffee can, knocked them out with fumes from rubbing alcohol and then tied strings around them."

"Strings?" Jillian frowned. "Why?"

"We had the bright idea of taking the other end of the strings and tying them around the door handle of the house. Soon the rubbing alcohol fumes wore off and there were four angry bees buzzing around the door handle. No one could get into the house or come out." He let out a low chuckle. "Boy was my mom mad."

She couldn't help but laugh, even as the sound ended in a yelp.

"That was the last shock. We're all finished," Cora announced.

Finally. Once Cora had removed the electrodes from her arms, Alec reached over to press her hand between both of his.

"Are you okay?" His expression was troubled.

She managed a nod. "Yes. But I'm glad it's over."

"I hear you." He leaned forward, placing her hand on the center of his chest, directly over his heart. "Feel my heart pounding? Even though I was trying to distract you with the boring story of my life, I swear I felt every one of those shocks as much as you did."

Looking at him more closely she could actually see small beads of sweat dotting his upper lip. Knowing he'd sat there, rambling about himself while empathizing with her as she endured the test, made her smile. "The bumblebee story was funny. Your life was far from boring, Alec." Her smile faded. "Having you here helped me more than I thought possible."

"I'm glad." He bent his head to kiss her fingers, but still didn't release her. "Remember that time you put all those stitches in me?"

She urged a brow. "Of course I do."

"You were there for me, too."

She frowned. "Stitching your wound was part of my job," she pointed out. As much as she liked knowing she had been there to take care of him, it wasn't the same situation at all. "You being here is very different."

"Maybe, but I'm glad you didn't have to go through this alone."

Unable to argue that one, she simply nodded. "Thanks, Alec."

"You are welcome." He grinned, as if trying to lighten the sudden seriousness between them. "How about if we go out for lunch? I'm hungry."

How could she refuse? She fingered the residual goop in her hair from the electrodes.

"Okay, but not until after I go home and shower."

"You look beautiful, as you always do." She wanted to laugh, but the intensity of his green gaze caught her off guard. Even though she knew better, she suddenly felt beautiful. Despite the copious amounts of white goop that had to be matted in her hair.

What was wrong with her? Being attracted to Alec wasn't part of the plan. Acting on that unmentionable attraction, like sharing another of those long, hot kisses, wasn't smart either. He and his daughter would be better off if she kept their relationship light, friendly.

Yet having him staying there with her, holding her hand and talking in that low, husky voice of his, was not exactly the path to a light friendship. He was the type of man who stood by a woman, in both good times and bad, offering his strength and support.

For the first time in her thirty-one years she realized just what her decision to dedicate her life to her career may have cost her.

ALEC PICKED Jillian up from her house and took her to his favorite Mexican restaurant. "What would you like to eat? Enchiladas? Chilaquiles? Carne asada tacos which are authentic Mexican tacos? Or my favorite chili Rellenos?"

She frowned as she scanned the menu, her freshly washed hair showing no trace of the white pasty stuff they'd used to attach the electrodes to her scalp. "I don't know, the chili Rellenos sound hot."

"They are. How about if we try a little of everything?" Taking the decision out of her hands, he ordered a large sampler platter, enough food to feed the entire emergency department.

After waitress hurried off with their order, he glanced at Jillian, his smile fading as he remembered how awful it had been to sit helplessly and watch while she suffered those electric shocks in silence. He could admit he'd been a little angry at the abrupt way she'd left Shannon's party, but then, when he'd gotten home from Chicago and had taken the time to listen to her voice mail message, he'd been relieved. Andrea had arched her brow when she'd heard the message and he'd inwardly groaned. Bad enough he'd had to sidestep Andrea's nosey questions about Jillian throughout the trip. Now for sure she wouldn't drop the subject.

Andrea had not understood the promise he'd made not to disrupt his daughter's life by bringing a woman into his relationship with his daughter.

Then again, seeing Jillian today, he was having trouble remembering why he'd made such a rash promise, himself.

The food didn't take long to arrive. Jillian sniffed the air appreciatively when their server arrived with her laden tray. "Wow. That smells delicious."

He had to restrain himself from leaning over to kiss her. He sat back to allow their server space to place the plates of food on the table. "Enjoy." she said with a wink.

They dug into the food with gusto. After a few minutes, Jillian asked, "Have you made any progress on the percocet case?"

He grinned as she took a large bite of her cheesy enchilada.

"Not much." The chili Rellenos were hot, just the way he liked them. He gulped some water, and then changed the subject. "When will you learn the results of your test?"

"I'm not sure." She dug into the chilaquiles with an enthusiasm that told him she'd been just as hungry as he. "You know," she mused with a tiny frown puckering her brow. "I was thinking about what you said, about the boy who was shot being a football player. It reminded me of how I treated a football player not that long ago, maybe a few weeks, because he'd severely strained his back during practice."

Spark of anticipation had him wishing he had his notebook on him. They could use a break in the case, as the hospital administrators had not gone along with the plan of installing a secret camera. At least, not yet. There had not been any more missing narcotics, either. The thief was obviously lying low for the moment. "Do you remember his name?"

Jillian bit her lip as she shook her head. "I don't remember, and I really couldn't tell you anyway, because of privacy rules. I do remember that I gave him a prescription for narcotics, though because along with his strained back we discovered he'd cracked a couple of ribs." She met his gaze. "Cracked ribs are extremely painful."

Her astute observations only helped to cement his theory. Now more than ever he was certain he was on the right track. "Do you remember anything else?"

"He was worried about how long I'd keep him on the injured reserve list." She shrugged. "He mentioned a big game coming up in October. I don't know the details, but maybe it was a game that would attract college scouts or something."

"Good point. I wonder if I can get a subpoena for his name." He figured it was worth a try. The phone in his pocket vibrated. Drawing it out, he recognized his sister's number. "Excuse me while I take this call."

"Of course."

"Hey, Andrea."

"Hi, Alec. Do you think you could pick up Shannon soon? Or do you want me to take her with me to Bethany's soccer game?"

"No, I'll pick her up in a few minutes." To his shame, he'd almost forgotten about the need to pick up his daughter by one o'clock. Thankfully, it looked as if Jillian was finished eating.

"Shannon?" Jillian guessed with a smile. He was relieved she didn't look annoyed.

"That's right. I need to pick her up from my sister's on the way home." He tucked his phone back into his pocket. "I hope you don't mind."

"Not at all."

Alec paid for their meal and then walked Jillian out to his car. She seemed lost in thought, and the way she worried her lower lip between her teeth made him want to cover her mouth with his to soothe her worries away. Only once he started, he wasn't sure he'd be able to stop.

Don't go there, he silently warned. She was off limits, remember?

"Are you working second shift again tonight?" Jillian glanced at him once they were seated in the car.

"Yes." He shot her a glance, as he headed for his sister's house. "You?"

"Same."

If he wasn't a father with a young daughter waiting for him at home, he might have suggested they get together for a drink after their respective shifts were over. But he was a father. Shannon would be up early. Besides, Megan the college student he'd hired to help him during the summer would also want to get home.

"I'm sure it's difficult for you to work second shift while Shannon is in school," Jillian said. "You probably don't see her much during the week."

"I switched to third shift after I brought Shannon home to live with me. My body didn't like working graveyard, but it was very nice to be home with her in the evenings. And I managed to get some sleep while she was at school during the day." Shannon was more important than his sleep schedule. "I'm next in line for the day shift, but if that doesn't happen by September, I'll have to go back to night shift." He would do whatever was necessary to care for his daughter.

Yet it occurred to him that if that happened, their schedules wouldn't match at all. It was yet another reason why a relationship between them would be impossible.

So why was he stuck on the idea of trying to make it work?

JILLIAN SHIFTED UNCOMFORTABLY in the passenger seat of Alec's car as he pulled into the driveway of his sister's house. She braced herself for more teasing. Would Andrea wonder what they were doing together? As it turned out, she needn't have worried because his sister along with the two girls were outside, waiting for them. Shannon ran over the minute they pulled up.

"Hi Daddy. Hi, Dr. Jillian."

"Hi yourself, munchkin." Alec didn't get out of the car, but simply waved at Andrea and Bethany, who was wearing a soccer uniform, while Shannon climbed into the back booster seat. He glanced over his shoulder, then began to back out of the driveway. "How was your morning?"

"Really fun. Beth and I played with our new dolls."

"Great." Alec grinned. We're just going to drive Dr. Jillian home, first, all right?"

"Actually, why don't you just head home?" Jillian suggested. She felt bad, keeping Alec away from the portion of the day he normally spent with his daughter. He'd been kind enough to come to her test, she didn't need to intrude on his personal time any longer. "I can walk from there."

"Yeah, Daddy. We can take Daisy and walk Jillian home again."

Alec nodded. "Fine with me."

When they reached Alec's house, Jillian had barely gotten out of the car when Shannon dashed past her toward the house to fetch her dog. In less than thirty seconds she'd returned with Daisy on her leash. The little dog wagged her tail with excitement and Jillian bent over to greet the cute pup.

"We're ready," Shannon announced.

Alec's phone vibrated again and he pulled it from his pocket. "I'm sorry, this is Rafe. Give me a few minutes, to take this."

She nodded. "Sure."

He lifted his phone to his ear and walked partially down the driveway, obviously looking for privacy. Maybe there had been some breaking news on their case. She wished he'd talk to her about it, but knew he wouldn't. Just as she couldn't breach patient privacy by giving him the name of the football player who'd sought treatment. Not that she could remember it anyway. She dropped down onto Alec's front stoop to wait.

"Sit here beside me, Shannon." Jillian patted the empty space. "Did you have fun at the doll store?"

"Yes. I got to spend the whole weekend with my daddy." Shannon dropped beside her but gazed after her father.

"I bet you miss him when he's at work," she murmured, noticing Shannon's wistful gaze.

The little girl nodded. "He has to work a lot."

"I know." She frowned. "But he still loves you."

"I love him, too." Shannon played with Daisy's leash, tugging to bring the dog back to them. "Dr. Jillian, is your job dangerous?"

"What?" For a moment the altercation she'd had with Barry Cox flashed in her mind, but she shoved it away. "No, of course not. Being a doctor is interesting, but not dangerous."

"My daddy's job is dangerous." Shannon bent over her knees to stare at her toes.

Uh-oh. Warning bells clamored in her mind. She glanced at the girl's bent head and asked, "Why did you ask that? Are you afraid for your daddy?"

"Sometimes." Shannon spoke in a muffled tone. Then she lifted her head to gaze up at Jillian. "I overheard Aunt Amber talking about my daddy's knife wound." Her brown eyes rounded. "Someone stabbed him!"

Yikes. She winced, knowing Alec wasn't going to like hearing that his daughter knew the truth. "Aw, sweetie, it's alright." She wrapped her arm around the little girl's thin shoulders and hugged her close. "Your daddy is a smart man. He knows how to be safe."

"I hope so." But the troubled expression in Shannon's eyes belied her words. The girl had already lost her mother, she knew better than anyone no one was one hundred percent safe all the time.

Jillian's heart broke for the little girl. "Shannon, you can talk to me anytime. I am always willing to listen. But if you're really afraid for your dad, maybe you should talk to him. I bet he'd like to know how you're feeling, too."

"I guess." Shannon's gaze focused at a point toward the driveway. Then she shot to her feet when Alec turned toward them. And just that quickly the moment was gone. "Daddy? Can we go now?"

"Yep." Alec held out his hand towards Shannon. His gaze met Jillian's. "Are you ready?"

"Absolutely." She stood and fell into step beside him. This wasn't the time to tell him about the little heart-to-heart she and Shannon had shared, but he should probably know about the little girl's fears.

They chatted about unimportant things, until they reached the foot of her driveway. She reached over to lightly clasp his hand. "Thanks for lunch."

His surprised gaze dropped for a moment to their joined hands, then back up to her face. "You're welcome."

Shannon was tugging on Daisy's leash, seeming not to be paying too much attention. "Um, do you think we could talk more, later?" She tried to tell him with her gaze that it was important.

"Sure." He didn't seem to get her silent message. "I'll give you a call."

"Great." She dropped his hand and turned to Shannon. "See you later."

"Goodbye, Dr. Jillian." Alec 's daughter surprised her by rushing over for a quick hug. She held the girl close suddenly glad she'd been there for her.

"Later." The glint in his green eyes made her feel better. Maybe he did understand that it was important for them to talk. She needed him to understand what Shannon was going through.

As she watched the pair walk away, the tall man with his little girl skipping beside him, she realized she deeply cared for Alec and Shannon.

Far more than she should.

CHAPTER NINE

A few hours later, Jillian gazed at the electronic census board, mentally ticking off the patients listed there. Yep, she'd seen all of those assigned to her block of rooms. It was time to wait for lab results, radiology results or for the next patient to be wheeled in. She was up for the first new admission.

Turning away from the census board, she noticed Lacy sitting alone in a corner of the nurses station, seemingly staring out at nothing.

Concerned, she crossed over. "Lacy? Are you okay?"

Lacy's gaze focused on her. "I guess." Her lack luster tone wasn't believable.

"Hey, I know it's been really stressful around here." She pulled up a chair so she could sit next to her colleague. "Things will get back to normal soon, you'll see."

For a moment Lacy's eyes filled with tears, then she quickly ducked her head and swiped at her eyes. "Sorry, I don't know what's wrong with me lately."

"Do you want to talk about it?" She searched Lacy's gaze.

"No." Lacy's smile was brittle. "Things won't get better until they catch whoever is stealing narcotics."

"I know." She could totally relate to how Lacy was feeling. "I hate knowing my name is on the long list of suspects, too."

"You?" Lacy scoffed and shook her head. "You have a stellar reputation around here. There isn't a single person who thinks you're guilty."

She wasn't so sure. And besides, it was clear when Chris had come to talk to her that he expected her to help resolve the issue. Talk about the burden of proof. "Maybe, but it still doesn't look good to have this going on while I'm the interim medical director."

"Tell me about it," Lacy said dryly. "Being the charge nurse isn't much easier."

Jillian didn't doubt it. This was what leadership was all about, taking responsibility for things you couldn't control.

Deep down, she knew Alec didn't believe she was guilty, yet he wasn't willing to discuss any of the details of the case with her. Yes, she understood his rationale, but still it rankled.

Her pager app went off, signaling their mini break was over.

"Come on," she told Lacy, rising to her feet. "We have a new patient on the way in."

There wasn't much time to dwell on Alec, although she did hope he'd stop by sometime to see her. Or, at the very least, call. The heavy burden of worry his daughter carried shouldn't be shouldered alone. Somehow, she had to convince Alec to talk to his daughter. It would be far better for Shannon to explain her feelings to him.

So much for her silent conviction to stay away from

him. It was proving to be more and more difficult to keep her thoughts from going back to Alec and Shannon.

Did she really need to stay away? Maybe her experience with relationships was nonexistent, but these feelings she harbored for Alec were worth exploring. And why couldn't she have both a family and a career?

Because she might have multiple sclerosis, that's why.

Her hope deflated like a punctured balloon. But then she tried to look on the bright side. If Dr. Juran didn't find anything wrong with her, there was no reason she couldn't find a way to balance family life with her career. Lots of people did it all the time. It's not like she would be the first.

A few minutes later her patient arrived, a seventeen-year-old young man with a possible head injury resulting in a seizure.

When the paramedics burst through the doors, she was shocked to discover Alec had accompanied the patient. Was this kid part of his percocet case? The patient was certainly large enough to be a football player.

Alec must have noticed the questions in her gaze. "His name is Frank Albert and he began having seizures when we questioned him."

She nodded, indicating she understood. "Lacy, make sure he has good IV access. Marianne, draw a drug screen to make sure he doesn't have narcotics in his system," she added.

Alec's expression was grim. "He had two percocets on him. You may want to get a CT scan of his head, too. He mentioned something about having a concussion after his last football practice."

She'd guessed right. Frank was a football player. If Alec found percocets on him, he must be involved in this mess, too. Helpless anger simmered in her stomach as she looked at the boy's young face. He might be a healthy, muscular kid, but he wasn't invincible, no matter what he might think. Had he taken the percocets to control the pain of his headache? At this point, until his drug screen came back, she was forced to assume so.

"I will." She stared at her patient, knowing he would be post ictal from the seizures, making his neural assessment useless. "Who intubated him?"

"The paramedics on the scene," Alec said. "He'd stopped seizing before they arrived. I held his head, keeping his airway open until they could get the tube placed."

Alec's past experience as a medic had saved this boy's life. His keen medical intuition was still on target. Ridiculously proud of him, she nodded. "Alright, let's get this kid to the CT scanner, STAT."

She turned and entered the order into the computer even as Lacy picked up the phone. Less than a minute later, Lacy turned toward her, her expression serious. "They're ready. I'll take him to radiology."

"Thank you." Jillian watched as Lacy quickly wheeled the patient down the hall, where the radiology department was located.

She turned back to Alec. "Did you learn anything from our patient before he began to have seizures?" She kept her voice low so no one else could overhear. "Did he tell you who gave him the pills?"

"No." Alec frowned. "I didn't learn as much as I would have liked. He admitted to taking the percocets, he actually threw them at me, claiming they didn't work anyway. Moments after that he fell to the ground in a full Grand Mal seizure. I suspect even percocets couldn't help the pain in his head if his head injury was getting worse."

"No, they would not work." The idea of someone taking

advantage of these kids by providing illegal drugs made her feel sick. "Sounds like he should have come in for treatment right away."

A dark shadow fell over Alec's eyes. "Yeah, no kidding. Makes me want to go have a chat with his coach."

She fell silent for a moment, wondering what Frank's CT scan would show. "He was lucky you showed up to question him."

"It was our second time through. I'm convinced the kids know something, but they aren't talking. The little bit Frank revealed was the first breakthrough we have. And that's not enough." He couldn't hide his frustration.

That was not good news. "I hope you get one of them to crack soon."

"We will. No matter what it takes." He sounded confident, looked almost invincible in his dark uniform, his shield and the gun on his hip.

He was very capable, yet she knew only too well he was flesh and blood beneath uniform. Hadn't she stitched him up once, already?

Didn't he realize just how worried Shannon was about his safety?

Glancing around to make sure she wasn't needed elsewhere, she lowered her voice. "Alec, I know it's none of my business, but maybe once this case is over you should consider finding a less dangerous job."

He stared, obviously shocked by her abrupt change in subject. "Why on earth would you say that?"

Her gaze skittered from his. "Think about the danger you're constantly exposed to. There must be other positions within the Milwaukee Police Department that would be less risky."

She forced herself to turn back to meet his gaze. For a

long moment they stared at each other without speaking. Jillian's heart sank as she realized he was not the least bit happy with her suggestion.

———

ANNOYED, Alec hated to admit she was right. Once he'd considered taking the sergeant's exam. But that had been a long time ago. Yet how he conducted his life wasn't any of her business. Why on earth had Jillian brought this up now? "I'm not really in that much danger. Smart cops enjoy long, healthy careers." It was true, yet there was no denying the current climate put cops in the center of danger more than ever before.

Jillian crossed her arms protectively over her chest, her gaze still troubled. "Shannon needs you, Alec. She's already lost one parent, she doesn't need to lose another."

Anger spiked, hot and swift. "I love my daughter. I'd never do anything to hurt her."

"Not on purpose," she agreed. "But don't you realize how much she depends on you?"

Yes, he did. He loved Shannon with his whole heart, but sometimes the realization of just how dependent she was on him for her well-being was scary. No matter what he did for a living, the responsibility of being a parent wouldn't go away.

Still, his career wasn't always dangerous and he refused to feel guilty for having a job he loved. He was about to say something more, when a horrible thought hit him. "Did Shannon tell you she was worried about me being hurt on the job?"

Jillian hesitated and then nodded in relief. "Yes. I'm sorry, I had to tell you. I don't want to break her confidence, but you need to talk to her, Alec. Somehow she overheard your family talking about your knife wound. She knows you were stabbed. She asked me about it."

His gut clenched. He hadn't wanted that fact to slip out. Troubled by the news, he slowly nodded. "I will talk to her. I don't want her to be afraid.

"I'm sure she's thinking the worst because she already lost her mother." Jillian might be trying to make him feel better but it wasn't working.

Because that was exactly the point.

This was why he'd promised not to make any changes that would upset Shannon. Only he hadn't really considered how his daughter would feel about his career.

"Dr. Davis? Your seizure patient is on his way back from the CT scanner."

"Thank you." She lightly squeezed his arm. "I'm sorry. I'm sure Shannon will feel much better after the two of you have a heart-to-heart."

"I hope so," he murmured, watching her walk away.

As Jillian headed over to meet her patient, he scanned the people working in the area, attempting to put names to faces from the list they'd compiled. He and Rafe had interviewed all the employees on the list and had four names that topped their list of suspects. There were three nurses had close ties to members of the Barclay Park football team. And one nurse had a sister who was in rehab for drug addiction.

Jillian would hate knowing a few of her coworkers were suspects. Especially because she worked with them every day.

He watched as Lacy wheeled Frank Albert back into his room. Jillian immediately stepped up to take over the patient's care, demanding a neurosurgery consult STAT.

"What's going on?" He edged closer.

"He has a major bleed into his brain." Her face was tense as she ordered medications he'd never heard of, like lasix and mannitol. "If they don't get him to the operating room, he'll die."

Stepping back, he gave Jillian and her staff plenty of room to work. He knew that if anyone could save this kid's life, it was Jillian Davis. He'd been impressed with her the first time he'd met her, and over these past few weeks he'd only grown more in awe of her talent and ability.

Once she'd finally gotten a hold of the neurosurgeon, he'd taken one look at the CT scan and then ordered the patient to be taken straight up to surgery.

Only after Frank Albert was taken away by the neurosurgery team did Jillian seem to remember he was there. She stepped back toward him. "They're going to operate. But his chances aren't great. The bleeding is really significant," she cautioned.

"I know." He didn't like the thought that this boy might be one of those kids they couldn't save. The ones he lost, haunted him. Now, and back when he'd been a medic, before they'd pulled him out to work as a sharpshooter. Being back here, he'd thought things would be better. Yet here he was, witnessing the loss of another young man.

With a grimace, glanced at his watch surprised to note it was barely eight o'clock PM. It seemed so much later. "I need to go. Rafe and I still have a long shift ahead of us."

"Are you okay?" Her questioning gaze sought his. He wasn't sure if she was referring to Frank's turn for the worse, or the revelation of his daughter's career concern.

"Yeah." Once he'd gotten over the shock of what Jillian had told him, he realized it was good to know how Shannon really felt. And he appreciated she'd cared enough to let him know.

"Jillian? Do you mind if I stop by later?"

She stared at him for a second or two and he wished he knew what she was thinking behind those sparkling blue eyes. Finally, she gave him a small smile. "I'd like that."

"Good. I'll see you later then." He watched as she crossed the room to where a patient was waiting to be seen. He loved how she looked so serious when taking care of her patients.

It reminded him how he'd found Shannon playing doctor with her dolls, including the newest one. Trust his daughter to take an expensive doll and wrap gauze around her head, making the doll into a patient. He knew lots of kids played doctor or nurse, but he couldn't help hoping this was a sign his daughter really would pursue a career in medicine. Jillian was a great role model for his daughter.

No way did he want Shannon to follow in his footsteps to become a cop. Just imagining his daughter learning to shoot a gun was enough to make his skin crawl.

Maybe Jillian was right. Maybe he really did need to consider a more stable, less dangerous career.

And as he headed back outside to meet Rafe, he wondered just what it meant that his daughter had chosen to confide in Jillian, rather than one of his sisters.

JILLIAN SAW several new patients and followed up on previous ones, but throughout the next few hours of her shift, Frank Albert dominated her thoughts.

When she couldn't stand not knowing how he was doing for a second longer, she logged into the computer and searched the operating room listing to see if Frank was still in surgery.

He was.

Reading further, she noted his blood pressure and his pulse remained sky high. He was getting plenty of medication to bring those levels down, which meant he would likely end up going to the neuro intensive care unit once the surgery was over.

She clicked out of his chart and sat for a moment battling despair. High blood pressure and pulse despite medications could be a sign of impending brain herniation. There was a very good chance Frank could die, despite the surgery he'd undergone. If only he'd sought medical treatment sooner, maybe his life wouldn't be hanging on by a frayed thread.

Pulling herself together, she stood and threw herself into work. There were plenty of other patients in the emergency department who were not hovering on the brink of death. Better for her to focus on helping those who needed her expertise rather than on those beyond her reach.

At least Alec hadn't been too upset about Shannon. He was the type of guy who would always put his daughter's needs first.

Not that she minded. His loving attitude toward his daughter was one of the things she admired most about him. Listening to Shannon describe her fears about her daddy being hurt had nearly made her cry.

The next few hours flew by. She made triage decisions, provided treatment and discharged patients to keep things moving.

At the end of her shift, Jillian took the elevators up to the fifth floor where the neuro intensive care unit was located. Her steps slowed as she approached Frank Albert's room.

Sobbing family members surrounded him at the bedside.

Feeling sick, she found the nurse. "What happened with Frank Albert?"

"He's not doing well." The nurse's eyes were suspiciously bright as if she'd shed a few tears with the family. "We're started the hypothermia protocol of course, but we've also prepared the family for the possibility brain death."

Her heart sank. Brain death was a difficult concept for some people to understand. When blood stopped going to the brain a patient was legally dead. In young patients, like Frank the heart and lungs continued beating for up to a day or two until the rest of the body died. The only good part about a patient who was declared brain dead was the ability for that patient to donate his organs to those in need. If the patient had indicated that was his or her wish, and if the family allowed.

That was a conversation the neuro intensive care team would have with his family. She tried not to go there. There was always a chance Frank would pull through, he was young, and otherwise healthy. The hypothermia protocol could work.

"Did you need anything else?" The nurse asked.

She shook her head. "Thanks for letting me know."

Turning on her heel, she returned back down to the emergency department, hoping more than anything that Alec had been able to stop by.

ALEC FINISHED HIS SHIFT, feeling bone weary and heart sick. Yet just the thought of seeing Jillian had perked him up. He debated going home to change his clothes, but didn't want to miss seeing Jillian. He also wanted to know how Frank Albert was doing.

Besides, if he went home, he'd have to explain to Megan, Shannon's babysitter, why he was changing his clothes and going back out. As if he didn't already feel guilty enough, sneaking over to see Jillian for a few minutes. It was silly to be worried, Shannon was sleeping and wouldn't miss him one little bit. Yet guilt nagged at him.

Throwing the gear shift into park he rested his forehead on the steering wheel. Was he crazy to have stopped by here? What if Jillian had to work late? How long would he stick around, waiting?

As long as it took to see her, he acknowledged grimly.

Man, he was in serious trouble. Considering the promise he'd made, he shouldn't be here. Yet that didn't stop him from sliding out from behind the wheel of his car to go inside. As he walked toward the entrance of the emergency department, he caught sight of Jillian walking out.

She had taken off her lab coat and had removed the band from her hair, so it flowed freely around her face. The moment he saw her, his heart skipped in his chest. Her gaze met his and he saw relief along with the shadow of grief, her lips trembling slightly as she tried to smile.

He quickened his pace as she continued walking toward him. She never hesitated when he hauled her close in a welcoming hug.

Neither of them spoke, yet they seemed to be connecting on a visceral level. He lowered his mouth to hers, and she eagerly met him more than halfway. Sizzling heat flared between them.

It seemed as if the past few weeks had been leading to this one particular moment. He kissed her as if he was starving, craving her in a way he hadn't wanted anyone else. When he managed to force himself to stop kissing her, he leaned his forehead against hers, breathing heavily. "Jillian." His voice held a ragged edge he couldn't hide. "I've missed you."

"I've missed you, too." She pulled away to look up into his eyes. The shadow of grief had returned and he instinctively braced himself for the worst. "I need to tell you that Frank Albert isn't doing very well. The bleeding in his brain is bad and there's a good chance he'll…" She didn't finish.

"I know." He'd secretly known this might be the outcome. When Frank had thrown the percocets at him, he'd suspected he'd been suffering bleeding into his brain for hours maybe even a couple of days. "I'm sorry, Jillian."

"Me, too." She buried her face against his neck. "Please, hold me."

"I will." He cradled her against his chest, wishing they could stay like this forever. But of course, they couldn't. "For now," he amended softly. He hadn't meant to hurt her, but when she stiffened in his arms, he knew he had.

He loosened his grip, letting her go. Jillian stepped back, avoiding his gaze.

He never should have come back here tonight, starting something he couldn't or wouldn't finish.

CHAPTER TEN

For now? Sharp disappointment stabbed deep. Until the moment Alec had caught her up in his arms, kissing her like there was no tomorrow, she hadn't realized just how much she needed this.

Needed him.

Because at this moment she didn't care about all the logical reasons she shouldn't be there with him. In the darkness it was too easy to imagine they were the only people on the face of the earth.

She had never been so attracted to a man before. Alec was the only one who had made her feel special. Desirable.

Something she hadn't felt in a very long time.

"I—feel the need to apologize," Alec's voice was low and husky. "I shouldn't have kissed you. I really need to go home to my daughter." He looked so miserable, her disappointment faded.

"Of course. I understand." And she did. She swallowed her regret, forcing a smile. The way he put his daughter first, was one of the things she admired about him.

He let out a long sigh. She forced herself to take a step

back, giving him room. She was about to turn away, when he reached out to grasp her arm.

"Wait a minute. What about Thursday?"

"Thursday?" She repeated, trying to understand what he was getting at. "What's special about Thursday?"

He flushed. "I just remembered, Shannon has a brownie Girl Scout day camp on Thursday. My sister Andrea is taking the girls and offered to keep Shannon overnight. I happen to be off that day, although I was considering an extra shift." He took a step toward her. "If you're free, I would love to take you out for dinner."

She hesitated, then nodded. How could she refuse? "I'm working day shift, Thursday so yes. I would love to have dinner."

"Thank you." Alec caught her in a quick hug. "I'll make reservations at DiCarlos Italian restaurant downtown. Will that work for you? It's a Monroe family favorite."

His eagerness made her smile. She nodded. "It's a date."

ALEC HAD TROUBLE FALLING ASLEEP, thoughts of Jillian had him tossing and turning for what seemed like hours before he finally succumbed to restless slumber. What seemed like five minutes later, Shannon and Daisy jumped into his bed to wake him up.

"Daddy, don't be such a sleepyhead!" No soft, gentle patting of his cheek this morning, Shannon bounced on the mattress, full of energy. "Wake up, Daddy! You promised to make French toast and bacon this morning for breakfast!"

Had he? He groaned. Must have sounded like a good idea at the time. Prying one eye open, he tried to read the screen of his alarm clock. Seven in the morning. It could have been worse. And that his lack of sleep was his own fault for kissing Jillian. Suppressing a pathetic moan, he pulled himself upright.

"I'm awake." Or he would be once he downed a full pot of coffee.

"Good!" Shannon scrambled off the bed and Daisy followed.

He stumbled to the kitchen, heading straight for the coffee maker as Shannon began to help assemble the ingredients for their breakfast. Despite his fatigue, he couldn't help but grin. Shannon's sunny disposition had a way of putting him in a good mood no matter what. It was something he hadn't appreciated before she'd come to live with him.

"What's so funny, Daddy?" Shannon asked, tilting her head to one side.

Realizing he probably looked like an idiot, grinning at her, he pulled himself together. "Nothing is funny, munchkin. I'm just happy."

"I like it when you're happy," Shannon announced.

Her innocent remark stopped him mid stride.

Shannon liked it when he was happy. Being with her made him happy. And so did being with Jillian. Yesterday Shannon had played doctor and had asked when they were going to see Jillian again. He'd mentioned going to the park over the weekend, promising to stop by to see if Jillian was home.

Was it possible he was making a big deal out of nothing? Eyeing his daughter, it was obvious Shannon had come a long way from the crying, and emotionally unstable little girl she'd been when he first brought her home. She'd blossomed over the past few months. Had settled into their new routine without too much trouble. His family had helped, but he'd made her his primary focus, too. Which was why he'd made that promise not to disrupt her life ever again.

Was it wishful thinking on his part, that the promise he'd made might no longer be needed?

There was no reason to think Shannon would be traumatized by his having a relationship with Jillian. If anything, his daughter would only benefit from the added security of a happy family.

Emphasis on family.

Shannon already used Jillian as a confidant. He still needed to sit her down to discuss her fears. But that aside, he noticed Shannon dropping hints on how much she wished she had a brother or sister to play with, like her cousin Bethany, who had a younger brother, Ben. Shannon would no doubt be delighted if he were to have a child with Jillian.

Whoa. What was he thinking? Marriage came before a family.

Marriage? Family? With Jillian?

A fist squeezed in his chest, making it hard to breathe. He set down his coffee without tasting a drop. Wide awake now, without the benefit of caffeine, he sank into the kitchen chair.

Somehow, without meaning to, he'd fallen in love with Dr. Jillian Davis.

JILLIAN OVERSLEPT ON THURSDAY MORNING. Unusual for her, as she happened to be a naturally early riser. Blame it on the fact that she hadn't been on a date in too many years to count.

The idea of having an entire evening alone with Alec

made her nervous. It occurred to her that dating a single father came with big responsibilities. She didn't want to hurt Alec or Shannon. What if things didn't work out between them? She couldn't bear the thought of making the little girl who had already lost so much, cry.

Okay, maybe she was over analyzing this. It was dinner. A simple date. Not a marriage proposal.

She quickly showered and blow dried her hair, wishing she didn't have to tie it back from her face while at work. As if Alec hadn't already seen her at her worst, she thought ruefully. She hurried to the kitchen to grab a bite to eat before heading to the hospital, when she noticed she'd missed a call. The number on her phone screen indicated the call had come from Trinity Medical Center.

She hesitated, debating the need to return the call. She was headed to the hospital anyway, whoever called could talk to her in person. Yet the call could be related to her role as the interim medical director. Stuffing a breakfast bar into her purse, she headed for the door, while calling the number back.

When the woman on the other end of the line announced she was from the neurology clinic, her body tensed. "Is this Jillian Davis?"

"Yes." Her voice came out in a hoarse croak, so she repeated herself. "Yes. This is Jillian Davis."

"My name is Barbara Evans, I'm a temp from the neurology clinic. I'm calling to let you know the results of your evoked potential tests were negative."

"Negative?" Jillian looked down at her hand wondering why she'd dropped the forceps the other day. Or why she was having numbness and tingling in her fingers. "Really?"

"Yes."

"But then what's causing my symptoms?" Jillian was

thrilled to know she probably didn't have multiple sclerosis, but that didn't mean there wasn't something else wrong with her.

"Oh, I'm sorry, I don't know about that. I will ask Dr. Juran to give you a call, okay? You can discuss your next steps with him."

"Yes. Thank you." She lowered her phone then lifted her gaze heavenward. God had been watching out for her, that was for sure. The negative result was good news. Certainly, something to celebrate.

Before she could talk herself out of it, she dialed Alec's number, determined to share the good news.

But he didn't pick up. She decided to leave a voicemail anyway. "Hey, it's Jillian. I just found out the results of my evoked potential testing is negative. Something to celebrate tonight. Can't wait to see you later, bye."

Feeling slightly foolish, she disconnected from the call. Maybe Alec wouldn't really understand the implications of her negative results, but that was okay. Having someone you cared enough about to share good news with was all that mattered.

Jillian drove to the emergency department for her early morning shift, already thinking about the evening to come.

AS SOON AS she arrived at work, Jillian realized her good mood was a bit premature. The atmosphere in the emergency department was tense. Not a single staff member was smiling. The easy camaraderie and light banter had vanished. Susan, the nurse taking care of one of her patients, looked particularly bad, her face pale and her sunken eyes surrounded by dark circles.

They were too busy with patients, so she didn't get a chance to talk to Susan until things quieted down, toward the end of their shift.

When she spied Susan sitting alone at one end of the nurse's station, she quickly crossed over. "Susan?" She hoped the nurse wasn't coming down with the flu or some other virus. "Are you feeling alright?"

Susan lifted her shoulder, but didn't meet her gaze, pretending to be engrossed in the chart open on the computer screen in front of her. "Fine."

Susan didn't look fine. She looked stressed. Or upset, as if she hadn't slept in a week. "Is something bothering you? I'm here if you want to talk."

"No." Susan was uncharacteristically abrupt, her closed expression didn't invite further discussion. Susan typed a brief note on the computer, then logged off. She jumped from her seat and walked away, her back stiff.

Surprised, Jillian watched her go.

"I heard the cops have been questioning her because her son plays for the Barclay Park football team." The knowing smirk on Wayne Netter's face made her want to slap him.

Yet the news still shocked her. Susan? The source of the narcotic thefts? No, she couldn't believe it.

As much as she would have liked to ignore Wayne, she needed to update him on the activities of the patients in their team. From the corner of her eye she caught sight of Alec, standing off in a corner of the emergency department. She was a little surprised to see him. She assumed he'd come and pick her up from her house, not from work. It made her smile to think he was as anxious as she was for their date. Yet, he didn't look impatient, quite the opposite. He leaned against the wall as if he had all the time in the world.

She sent Alec a give-me-a-minute smile and turned to Wayne. "Let's walk over to the census board. I'll give you a brief rundown on the patients and their dispositions."

"I'm sure I can figure it out on my own," he sneered. "I don't need your help."

She stared at him for a long moment, trying to understand what was at the root of his nasty tone. Then she decided to ignore him, turning back to the census board. She spoke, without caring if he listened or not. "There are two patients still waiting for diagnostic testing to determine their disposition, Jennifer Walden in room 21 and mark Robbins in room 18."

She was determined to give Wayne a concise report on their patients so he couldn't claim down the road that something was her fault because she hadn't given him some bit of information. She didn't trust Wayne as far as she could spit.

"You'll need to check their radiology reports before they can be cleared. There are three patients currently on the admission list waiting for inpatient beds. And there are four more patients we are waiting for lab results on." She swung back to meet his board gaze. "Any questions?"

"No." He turned on his heel and walked away. For a moment she marveled at his rudeness, then shook off her irritation. No way would she let Wayne's crankiness ruin her evening.

She was free to go.

In her office, she picked up her purse, then left, locking the door behind her. She returned to the emergency department to find Alec was still waiting in the same spot, leaning against the wall. He straightened when she approached.

"Hi." She tried not to sound as awkward as she felt.

"Hi, yourself." He grinned and she immediately relaxed when he pulled a bouquet of daisies out from behind his back. "I don't know what your favorite flower is, but these were growing in my garden. I hope you don't mind. Shannon helped me pick them."

She could easily imagine his daughter helping him to pick flowers for their date. It was probably the sweetest thing anyone had done for her. Burying her nose in the blossoms, she took a deep breath. Then looked up at him. "Thank you, Alec, they're beautiful."

He pulled her into his arms for a quick kiss. "You probably deserve orchids or roses, but I didn't have any of those in my garden. Since we're celebrating, I wanted to stop by to check in on you. I wasn't sure if you wanted to go home to change first before we head downtown to DiCarlos."

His comment about orchids or roses surprised her, neither were her favorite. But she decided it didn't matter. "I would like to go home to change, if you don't mind." The fact that he'd come here to surprise her with flowers, was touching.

"Great. Then I'll meet you at your place." He grinned and turned to head back to his car.

The ride from the medical center to her house didn't take long. She pulled into the driveway, then gathered her purse and her bouquet of daisies. She pushed open the car door and stepped out only to find Alec standing there ready to help. She flushed at his attentiveness.

"Thank you." She used her key to unlock the door then stepped inside. After taking a moment to put the daisies in water, she disappeared down the hall to her bedroom to change her clothes.

She'd agonized a bit over what to wear. It was a date, not a formal event. She finally settled on a yellow sun dress. Not too fancy and not too casual, she decided.

When she returned to the kitchen, she blushed when Alec gave her an admiring look. "Wow. You look beautiful."

"Um, thank you." She was so out of practice, it wasn't funny. Since when was dating this difficult?

Only when it mattered, she quickly realized.

"Are you ready to go?" Alec asked.

She managed a nod, picking up her purse from the table. Always the gentleman, Alec opened the door for her so they could step back outside. Then he jogged around to open the passenger door of his car, too.

As she slid into the passenger seat, she subtly pressed a hand to her stomach, trying to settle her nerves.

"I know it's a bit early," Alec said as he settled in behind the wheel. "I thought we could take a little walk down by the lakefront first, before dinner." He flashed a dazzling smile. "If you don't mind."

"That sounds wonderful." Instantly, she relaxed, understanding that there was no pressure here. Just his intent to show her a nice time.

She wasn't sure why, but being with Alec felt right.

CHAPTER ELEVEN

As he drove downtown to DiCarlos' restaurant, Alec tried to think of something to say. At one time, women had flocked to him, and he hadn't hesitated to enjoy himself. Case in point—Shannon. He shouldn't have been so irresponsible, but he couldn't regret having his daughter.

Just the circumstances, maybe. But as he was often reminded in church, God was in charge and everything happened according to His plan.

He'd changed his life one hundred and eighty degrees over the past nine months. And if he were honest, he'd admit that none of the women he'd dated before ever meant as much to him as Jillian. Although really, she could have any man she wanted. Why would she want to be with him?

Enough. He was driving himself crazy. She was here with him now, and that was all that mattered.

"How was work?" He mentally winced at the inane question.

"Busy as usual." She hesitated. "The staff were far more subdued today, even angry after being interviewed by the police."

He grimaced. "I'm sorry about that. It's unfortunate that we have to question everyone in order to uncover the truth."

"I know." She smiled sadly. "I just miss the camaraderie we once shared. The narcotic thefts have destroyed that feeling of teamwork."

"It's never easy to know you're working with a thief." Alec glanced at her. "I'm sure the staff are all staring at each other, wondering which one is guilty."

"They are." She sighed. "And others are gossiping about it, as well. Too bad Wayne Netter's name wasn't on the list. No one would miss him if he was arrested for the crime."

He frowned. "Has he been bothering you again? My youngest sister, Amber had trouble with a doc last year, and the hospital forced him out of his position."

"Really?" She sounded surprised. "He must have done something big, then. Most doctors are not let go because they are jerks."

"I guess not." He hated knowing this Netter guy was giving Jillian a hard time. "Have you ever been to DiCarlos?"

"Never." She smiled. "I'm sure it will be wonderful."

The tension eased, and soon they were chatting about other stuff. His family, and hers. Although hearing about how she lost both of her parents was heartbreaking. He couldn't imagine not having his parents in his life. Abe and Alice Monroe were celebrating forty years of marriage in a few weeks and the kids had banded together to throw them a party.

One he hoped Jillian would attend with him.

Was it too soon to ask? Maybe. This was only their first date.

Although he felt as if he'd known Jillian for months.

He pulled up in front of the restaurant, using the valet

parking since he knew there wasn't much general parking available especially in summer. The walk to the lakefront didn't take long. The beach was packed with people, and he grinned when he saw a rousing game of sand volleyball. Once he'd have jumped in to play.

"Looks like fun," Jillian said.

"Do you play?" He sent her a sly grin. "We Monroe's tend to be on the competitive side."

"Why doesn't that surprise me?" She asked, rolling her eyes.

After an hour of walking, they headed back to the restaurant. The atmosphere inside was romantically cozy. As they took their seats, he leaned forward. "This was where my sister Amber and her husband Nick had their first date."

"Really?" She eyed him curiously. "How long ago was that?"

"Last summer. They were married back in April." He turned his attention to the menu. "From what Amber said, everything here is delicious."

Their server brought a plate of appetizers. It was oddly romantic to share them with Jillian. He was in over his head but didn't care enough to save himself.

"I know you don't want to talk about the case," Jillian said.

He held up his hand to stop her. "I really can't. Please don't ask me to."

"Okay." She sat back in her seat. "But will you do one thing for me?"

"Like what?" he asked warily.

"Will you let me know if you're about to make an arrest." When he didn't answer, she added, "I'm the interim medical director of the emergency department. All I'm asking for is a heads-up if you're about to take one of the staff into custody. It's going to impact everyone, and I don't want patient care to suffer."

He could see why she'd want to be prepared for that. "Yes," he agreed. "I'll let you know."

"Thank you." Her smile was bright, as if he'd promised her the moon and the stars.

They lingered over their meal. Jillian had shared her salmon with him, and he'd offered her a bite of his tenderloin. With regret, he signaled for the bill.

The hour wasn't that late, and he purposefully took a drive along the lakeshore before heading home. As much as he didn't want the night to end, he knew they both had to work the next day.

She glanced at him in surprise when he pulled into his driveway. As if he had something more planned than dinner. He quickly reassured her. "Don't worry, I was hoping you wouldn't mind if I walked you home."

Before she could answer, his phone rang. He was tempted to ignore it. Rafe could wait.

"Shouldn't you get that?" Jillian asked.

His phone dinged with a text. He grimaced when he saw it was from Andrea.

Call me!

He did. "What is it? Shannon?"

"Yes, I'm sorry Alec, I'm on my way to your house right now. Shannon is sick with the flu. She wants to come home."

"Of course." He pushed out of the car, in time to see headlights approaching. "I'm here."

"I see you. Thanks." Andrea disconnected from the call. He stood for a moment, ashamed to realize he hadn't even considered the call to be about Shannon. His thoughts had gone straight to work.

He shouldn't have forgotten, even for a nanosecond that he had a daughter who needed him.

JILLIAN WAS KEENLY aware of Andrea's curious gaze as she handed a pale and tearful Shannon over to Alec.

"She feels warm," Alec said with a frown.

"Daddy, I'm sick," Shannon mumbled, lifting her head from his shoulder. "I don't like throwing up."

"I know, munchkin. No one likes to be sick." Alec cradled her close. "It's okay, you're home now."

"I hate to dump her on you, but I need to get back." Andrea sighed. "I'm sure it's just a matter of time before Bethany starts throwing up too."

"Thanks, Andrea."

His sister raised a hand before slipping back behind the wheel.

"Daddy, my tummy hurts again." Shannon's tone turned into a whimper.

"Do you have a bucket?" Jillian feared Shannon was going to throw up again. "And some towels?"

"In the basement, I think." He glanced at her. "Would you mind coming inside for a few minutes?"

"Of course."

They headed inside and Alec walked into the living room to place Shannon on the sofa.

"I'll stay with her," she offered. He flashed a quick smile, then retreated to find the bucket and towels.

Jillian settled beside Shannon, smoothing a hand down her back. The little girl was warm, likely running a low-grade fever. The little girl looked miserable and leaned her head against Jillian. "It's okay, your daddy will be back soon."

"My tummy hurts." She could tell the little girl was having stomach cramps by the way she clutched her belly and leaned harder against Jillian. If Alec didn't hurry, this poor child was likely to throw up all over his sofa.

"I know, sweetie." Jillian continued to soothe Shannon.

"Found one." Alec set the bucket on the floor and spread the towel out on an empty part of the sofa. He lifted Shannon up and set her on the towel, tucking the bucket close. "Hang on, I'll be right back." He disappeared down the hall, returning a few minutes later with a pillow.

"Daddy," Shannon murmured. She lifted her arms so that he picked her up into his arms and settled back on the sofa. He gave Jillian an apologetic glance, clearly regretting the way their evening had come to an abrupt end.

It certainly wasn't his fault.

Shifting Shannon to one side, he reached out and gently squeezed her hand. "I'll call you," he said in a low voice.

She nodded and rose to her feet. She tried to smile as she crossed the room and headed outside, leaving him alone with Shannon. She stood for a moment, feeling bereft. Which was silly. It really wasn't that late for her to walk home alone. Yet she also knew that if Alec had been with her, he would have kissed her goodnight.

Her walk home was uneventful. Yet she felt unsettled. Why, she wasn't sure. When she entered her house, the cheerful daisies made her smile. And that's when she realized what was bothering her.

She'd wanted to stay, to help take care of Shannon. But that possibility had not seemed to enter Alec's mind. It was almost as if he wanted to keep their personal romantic relationship separate from his daughter.

———

ALEC SAT BESIDE HIS DAUGHTER, staring down at her sleeping face. After she'd gotten sick one more time, she'd finally fallen into a restless sleep. He'd cleaned up the mess, gaining a new appreciation for what his parents had gone through with having six kids.

Total madness, he silently admitted. And while he loved his siblings, he had no idea how his parents had managed.

He hated knowing he'd forgotten his responsibilities of being a father. He'd assumed Shannon would be fine with his sister and her cousin Bethany.

Selfishly, he hadn't wanted his evening with Jillian to end. At least, not like this. Their walk on the lakeshore, their romantic dinner together hadn't been enough. He'd wanted to walk her home.

To kiss her goodnight.

Should he have asked her to stay? No, Jillian wouldn't want to come down with whatever bug Shannon had caught. And he would never take advantage of Jillian by making her sit with his sick daughter all night.

Besides, Jillian had to work the next day, as he did. Although now that he thought about it, he might need to call off work, staying home to take care of Shannon. Unless she was feeling better. And if Megan wouldn't mind staying. Either way, it wasn't Jillian's role to be a surrogate parent to his daughter.

Yet, as he listened to Shannon's even breathing, he

stared at the ceiling and thought about how nice it would have been to have Jillian there for emotional support.

Spending the time together, as if they were a family.

———————

THE NEXT DAY, Jillian heard from Alec just as she was about to leave the house for her shift at the hospital. She had switched a while ago to work the evening shift, which she now regretted as Friday nights we're typically insanely busy.

"Hi, Alec." She was glad he'd called as promised. "How is Shannon?"

"Better. She hasn't thrown up in almost five hours." Alex sounded tired—she imagined he hadn't gotten much sleep. "If she keeps down the chicken soup and toast I've given her for lunch, I may still make it to work."

"Kids tend to bounce back after illnesses much faster than adults," she agreed. "If she can keep food down, she'll be fine."

"I'm really sorry, Jillian," Alec said in an apologetic tone. "I feel awful our night ended so abruptly."

"Hey, it's not as if you planned for Shannon to get sick. I understand. Besides, I'm the one who forgot to thank you for dinner." She smiled, even though he couldn't see her. "I had a lovely time."

He sighed. "You're being awfully nice, but I do appreciate you understanding. The other reason I called is because Rafe has gotten a break in the case. I wanted you to know ahead of time that things might be crazy for a while."

She was touched that he'd cared enough to let her know about his busy schedule. "I hear you." She really wanted to know more but swallowed the questions formulating in her mind. He would call with an arrest as he'd promised, she couldn't ask for anything more. Susan, the nurse whose son was on the Barclay Park football team, looked as if she couldn't take much more. As tense as the atmosphere was in the emergency department, she hoped Alec and Rafe would find the guilty person soon.

"I was wondering if you we're busy this weekend. We're having a family barbecue at my parents' house on Saturday afternoon. If you're not working, we would love to have you join us."

She caught her breath at his invitation, knowing that if she agreed to go, there would be no hiding their relationship. As if Andrea had already seen them together already, she silently admitted. But this was Alec's way of including her in the warm embrace of his family. She'd met the Monroes once before. A second date would seal her status as Alec's girlfriend. What she ready for that?

"Thanks, I'd love to." The words popped out of her mouth before she could call them back.

"Great." Relief was evident in his tone. "I'll be in touch later with the details."

"Sounds good." She disconnected from the call, realizing she'd just taken a gigantic step toward admitting to the rest of the world how much she cared about Alec. Doubt fluttered in her stomach, but she pushed the butterflies away with determination.

There was really no reason she couldn't have it all. A career and a family. A beautiful stepdaughter.

And, most importantly, Alec.

THINGS WERE quiet until about nine o'clock that night, then the gates opened and a flood of patients poured in.

Just as she'd predicted.

Jillian dealt first with two victims of a motor vehicle crash. Thankfully, they were both wearing their seat belts, so their injuries weren't as bad as she'd expected. A few broken limbs were nothing compared to massive head and chest injuries.

The numbness and tingling sensations had returned to her right hand. When the traction bar had slipped from her fingers, thankfully bouncing harmlessly off the mattress of the bed, she'd been forced to step back and let the nurses finish setting it up.

Once she'd gotten the two patients admitted to the orthopedic trauma service, she received another call about a drug overdose. Ignoring her concern over the symptoms in her right hand, she headed back to the trauma bay. The cleaning fluid on the floor wasn't even dry when the double doors of the ambulance bay slammed open yet again.

The patient was a seventeen-year-old male, and she immediately thought of the Barclay Park football team. When Alec came in with the teenager, she knew with a sinking sensation this wasn't a typical overdose.

"We found empty percocet wrappers in his bedroom. We've given him two doses of Narcan on the ride over, but his pupils are still fixed and dilated." Alec's expression was grim, and she was not surprised to see their patient had the muscular build of an athlete. "The paramedics intubated him, but he needs a nasogastric tube to get activated charcoal."

If this situation wasn't so serious, she'd smile at how Alec was giving her orders on how to treat their patient. Instead, she focused on the young man. "How long ago did he take the medications?" She did a quick neural exam of her own. "Lacy, will you please get me a nasal gastric tube?"

"We don't know," Alec admitted. "His mother hadn't seen him for several hours."

Several hours wasn't good. Lace swiftly handed over the nasal gastric tube and Jillian pulled on a second pair of gloves before preparing to insert it.

She managed to get the tube halfway down, but then her fingers fumbled. Gritting her teeth, she tried to use her left hand to advance the tube. Then suddenly Alec was there, reaching over to help her. With his hands over hers, they advanced the tube to their patient's stomach. Moments later, Lacy verified the placement of the tube, and then gave the first dose of charcoal.

"Thank you, Alec," she whispered. There wasn't time for her to say anything more because her attention was needed for their patient.

"I have the results of his drug screen," William announced. "Positive for codeine."

Percocets had codeine in them so that confirmed what he'd taken. Was this an accidental overdose? The boy still hadn't woken up and that was more concerning than anything else.

It wasn't until she was unable to squeeze the ambu bag to give the boy deep breaths as they wheeled him up to the ICU, that Jillian realized her hand was much worse than before.

Her evoked potential tests may have been negative, but there was still something very wrong. And deep down she couldn't help but think it was serious.

In that moment she knew she couldn't go with Alec to his parents' house this weekend. Not until she knew for sure what was wrong with her. She never should have gotten so involved with Alec and his daughter. Shannon had already confided in her, had been comforted by her when she was sick. If Jillian continued to see Alec and Shannon, the little girl might view her as a mother.

She knew it was likely the little girl may see Jillian like that already. And that wasn't fair.

After the way Shannon had lost her mother to a non-curable illness, she couldn't bear the thought of putting the little girl through such heartfelt bereavement all over again.

CHAPTER TWELVE

During the rest of her shift, Jillian tried not to think about Alec and Shannon. But concentrating on work wasn't helping either. The whole emergency department was upset about the boy, Daniel McNeil, who'd overdosed on percocets. His neurological status had been bad, making his prognosis grim. She silently prayed Alec hadn't found him too late.

Frank, their previous patient, was still holding his own. The hypothermia protocol seemed to be working. For that she was grateful. But losing even one young man was one too many.

Alec had gotten another call and left right after she transferred Daniel to the ICU so she didn't get a chance to talk to him about how he'd found the boy. Or anything else, like the fact that she changed her mind about his invitation. Her stomach twisted, making her feel sick.

Thinking about Daniel was only slightly better than dwelling on her health. The idea of being diagnosed with the debilitating illness wouldn't leave her alone. Sitting in her office at the end of her shift, she stared at her hands.

No way around it, she'd have to get in touch with Dr. Juran again, and soon. It was Friday night, so she'd have to wait until Monday. The weekend stretched long and empty before her, especially now that she decided not to go to Alec's parents' house for the barbecue.

The pager app on her phone went off and she looked at the number with a sense of dread. Alec. What could she say to him? She wished she could tell him the truth. Knowing Alec, he'd come right over, take her into his arms and tell her everything would be alright.

Except she really didn't believe that. Oh, Alec would come, but it was the part of everything being all right that she didn't believe.

Swallowing against the lump in her throat, she dialed his number. "Alec? This is Jillian."

"Are you still at the hospital?" He sounded surprised.

"Yes." Her vision blurred and she forced herself to continue. "I'm sorry but I don't think I'll be able to get away tonight."

"I understand, although I would love to see you even just for a few minutes." He sounded disappointed and she hadn't even told him about the weekend yet. "I need to go home, though to check on Shannon. I talked to Megan earlier, and she said Shannon was doing okay, but I'd like to see for myself."

"That's only natural." She bit her lip and blinked away the tears. "We can talk another time, Alec. Give Shannon a hug for me."

"I will. Jillian, I uh..." he stopped, and then said, "Never mind. I'll talk to you tomorrow."

"Goodbye, Alec." She quickly ended the call before she started sobbing in earnest. Taking several deep breaths, she fought off the wave of depression and stood. Daniel

McNeil. She needed to focus on something besides her own misery. Daniel's life was on the line, she needed to go up to the ICU to check on him.

Anything was better than going home to her empty house. Alone.

ALEC GAZED at his sleeping daughter, relieved when it seemed she really was much better. According to Megan, her fever had broken about eight o'clock that evening and she hadn't thrown up during the entire time he was gone at work. He felt certain that Shannon would be back to her old self, wide awake and raring to go, by morning.

His smile faded. Shannon would be fine, but he couldn't say the same about Daniel McNeil. Too bad he hadn't found him sooner. In some ways it was a miracle he'd found the kid at all. He and Rafe had sensed a change in some of the football player's attitudes since the news of Frank's hospitalization had hit the streets. They'd discovered Daniel was the unofficial captain of the team, the one who scheduled group weight training sessions and held study hours for anyone having trouble memorizing the various plays. Daniel was not just the quarterback of the team but, according to the rest of the players, he was the heart and soul of the group.

Alec had been convinced Daniel would tell them the truth behind the percocets.

Instead, they'd found him unconscious, having accidentally or purposefully overdosed on them.

His mother had sworn the boy wasn't depressed. There was no suicide note, and his mother claimed Daniel was thrilled to be the first-string quarterback. He was really hoping for a college scholarship next year and his mother seemed to think there was a good chance he'd get it.

But not anymore. Even if Daniel woke up from his drug overdose, he'd likely not play anytime soon.

This whole percocet situation had spiraled out of control. The kid had almost died, could still die, just because someone was greedy enough to prey a player's willingness to do anything to be noticed. He'd never seen anything like it. Drugs in any form—narcotics or steroids—were bad news.

At first Daniel's mother hadn't wanted them to talk to her son, but when they pressed she'd reluctantly agreed. When she hadn't been able to wake Daniel, she began screaming his name. Alec and Rafe had rushed into the bedroom, and he had instinctively known time was of the essence. Rafe had called 911 while Alec had given first aid, holding the young boy's airway open and breathing for him until the ambulance had arrived.

The empty percocet wrappers they'd found had been buried in the bottom of the kid's garbage can. When they'd questioned Daniel's mother about them, she'd been shocked to see them. She had admitted Daniel had suffered a shoulder injury that impacted his throwing arm. But she hadn't thought the injury bad enough to interfere with his playing. The additional information convinced Alec that this was likely an accidental overdose. Not a suicide attempt.

Yet the end result was the same.

Alec turned away from his sleeping daughter, still seeing Daniel's unresponsive face in his mind. He'd requested the paramedic to give the boy Narcan, the antidote to narcotics, but even two doses hadn't worked. Because Daniel had been too far gone? He didn't know and could only hope the charcoal had been able to bind to the medication enough to do some good.

That train of thought led him right back to Jillian. Her fingers appeared to be bothering her again. He'd noticed she'd had difficulty placing the nasal gastric tube, so he'd given her a hand. Thankfully his medic training had prepared him well. Placing nasogastric tubes wasn't difficult. He'd done far more technical procedures when he'd been in the army.

He sank on the sofa, scrubbing his palms over his eyes. Daniel's face, and those of the other kids he'd lost, swam through his mind. He'd thought as a police officer in the civilian world he'd have a chance to help people, but most of the time he felt like he was only getting further behind. First there had been Ricky, who died of a gunshot wound. Then Frank had ended up in the ICU. Now Daniel.

His goal had been to make the world a safer place to live, especially for kids. He felt more strongly about his mission now that he had Shannon.

He stared at his silent television, wishing Jillian was there with him. Should he call her again? No, she sounded pretty dejected when they'd spoken earlier. Given the critical nature of Daniel's condition, he couldn't blame her. And he couldn't help wondering if she was concerned about her hand. She'd told him the tests were negative, but obviously something was wrong. Tomorrow, he decided. He'd call her tomorrow and take her to his parents. There was nothing like a Monroe family event to lighten the mood. And since Shannon would be preoccupied with Bethany and Ben, he and Jillian may be able to find some time to talk alone.

At least, he hoped so.

THE NEXT MORNING, Shannon woke him by bouncing on the bed. It had been cute the first time she'd done it, but now he swallowed a low groan. At least his daughter must be feeling better. He roused himself, flashing Shannon a big grin.

"What would you like for breakfast this morning?"

"Daisy and I want to go for a walk in the park," Shannon announced. "You promised."

His daughter liked to use his own words against him. Had he promised? It seemed these days he was breaking his promises more than he was keeping them. Especially the big one of not causing upheaval in Shannon's life. Stifling a sigh, he headed for the kitchen. "We'll go to the park after breakfast."

"Now, Daddy." Shannon planted her hands on her slim hips, her lower lip thrust forward.

He was not going to the park until he had something to eat and had showered. If they ran into Jillian, he didn't want to look like something dragged through the mud. "Shannon." He used his stern father's warning tone so she would understand he was serious. "We are going to eat breakfast, first. Do you want cereal or eggs?"

His daughter's gaze narrowed into a mutinous glare and he was struck by how much she reminded him of himself at her age. Swallowing another sigh, he realized his parents were true saints for raising six kids, most of them boys. For all the trouble he'd gotten into as a kid, he could appreciate how fortunate it was that he'd grown up in a large family.

And for the first time, he realized he wanted the same thing for his kids.

When his daughter didn't respond, he made the decision for her by going to the fridge for eggs. After a few minutes Shannon flopped into a chair, her chin practically dragging on her chest as he whipped up a batch of scrambled eggs and toast.

Her attitude had mellowed by the time he set a plate in front of her. She dug into the meal with enthusiasm. When she'd finished, in record time, her expression was hopeful. "Now can we go to the park?"

"As soon as I wash the dishes and shower," he promised, carrying his dirty dishes to the sink. "And don't say it," he warned, lifting his hand to stop her when she opened her mouth. "You need to learn to be patient. It only takes me five minutes to do the dishes and another fifteen to shower and shave. Surely you can wait that long."

"I guess," she said with a long-suffering sigh, as if he'd asked her to wait fifteen hours instead. "But will you at least hurry?"

He rolled his eyes and turned to wash the dishes, leaving them in the sink to air dry. Then he headed for the bathroom. He really did hurry, which was ridiculous considering he'd just lectured his daughter on the merits of patience. Yet he couldn't deny he was anxious to see Jillian again. He'd planned to call her, but chatting in person would be better.

Shannon was waiting outside, Daisy already clipped to her leash by the time he emerged from his room, dressed in soft denim jeans and a blue and gray striped polo shirt. The barbecue at his parents didn't start until two o'clock that afternoon, so they had plenty of time. He and Shannon walked Daisy all around the park, laughing when the dog tried to chase the birds.

It was close to ten-thirty in the morning before they'd made their way to the other side of the park closest to

Jillian's house. Even though Alec knew he'd see Jillian later, he walked up to the front door and knocked.

He frowned when no one came to the door. He knocked again, louder, in case she hadn't heard him, but after a few minutes he swallowed his disappointment and drew Shannon away.

"She's probably still sleeping—we'll see her later," Alex said in a cheerful voice. Jillian's shift had probably gone later than planned. And she was no doubt tired. "Come on, I'll race you and Daisy home."

Shannon let out a shriek and took off at a run, Daisy's short legs galloping madly to keep up. He slowed his pace to let Shannon win the race as they neared home.

He waited until noon to call Jillian. When she didn't answer, he left a quick message, asking her to return his call. After another thirty minutes had passed, he paged her.

Pacing the length of the kitchen, he battled frustration when she didn't immediately return his call. What had happened? Was she still sleeping? Or had she changed her mind? It wasn't as if this was the first time she'd meet his family—the whole clan had been there for Shannon's birthday.

When his cell phone rang he was so startled he almost dropped it. Quickly he answered. "Hi Jillian."

"Hi back." Her voice sounded nasal, stuffed up as if she had a bad cold. "I'm sorry but I'm not feeling well. I think it's better if I stay home rather than pass my germs along to your family."

He ignored the sharp stab of disappointment. "You sound awful. What can I do? Shannon and I can bring over some chicken soup," he offered.

She sniffled loudly and for a moment it sounded as if she were crying. "No, I don't want either of you to get sick, but thanks for the offer. I'm sorry. Hopefully I'll feel better in a few days."

"I hope so, too. Take care of yourself." He forced cheerfulness into his tone to mask his mood. There were a lot of summer bugs going around. First Shannon had come down with the flu now Jillian had a cold. He should be grateful he was feeling fine, but knew if it were only him, he'd take the risk and go visit Jillian. Dejected, he set his cell phone aside and looked at his daughter. "Jillian is sick, so you and I are on our own for the barbecue."

"Oh, that's not good." She looked as disappointed as he felt. "But it's okay, Daddy. We'll have fun anyway, right? I'll keep you company so you're not lonely."

Her comment stunned him. Did Shannon realize how important Jillian was to him? He wouldn't be surprised if she did. His young daughter was amazingly astute, especially when it came to reading other people's feelings. He drew her in for a quick hug.

"I love you, Shannon," he said in a husky tone. "And don't worry about me. I'm not lonely now that I have you. You and I will be just fine together."

"Yep," Shannon readily agreed. "Because we're a team, right Daddy? We are part of the A-Team."

"Right." He smiled and kissed the top of her head.

But later that day, while he was truly enjoying himself at his parent's barbecue, he couldn't help the pang of regret when Amber asked about Jillian.

Because even though he loved his daughter, there was a tiny part of him that longed for something more than just being a parent.

Shannon was important, his daughter meant the world to him, but so did Jillian.

Now that he'd had a taste of what it would be like to

have a family, a true partnership like his parents, he wouldn't be satisfied with anything less.

He wanted that family and partnership with Jillian.

JILLIAN BURIED her head in her pillow, stifling her uncontrollable sobs the best she could. Despair filled her heart all the way down to her soul, grieving for something she couldn't have. After several long minutes she managed to get herself under control. No easy feat as she'd been fighting this battle all day, going through crying jags since earlier that morning, after she'd gotten off the phone with Dr. Juran.

Her symptoms hadn't gone away overnight and when she'd gotten up, the thought of waiting until Monday to talk to Dr. Juran had seemed impossible. So she'd paged the neurology specialist directly, not sure if he would answer when he wasn't on call.

He did. And he listened intently as she described how the symptoms were worse. How she couldn't squeeze an ambu bag to breathe for a patient, neither could she place a nasal gastric tube.

"Your temporary assistant called to tell me the evoked potential tests were negative, so what in the world is wrong with me?" she'd asked with agonizing frustration.

There had been a long silence and her stomach had clenched painfully.

"I'm sorry, Jillian. The temp got the test results mixed up. Your evoked potential testing wasn't negative."

Dear Lord have mercy she thought as she sank into a chair. "They weren't?"

"No. I don't like to give this sort of information over the

phone, but I'm afraid you are in the very early stages of multiple sclerosis. The good news is that your symptoms are mild and there's a new medication regime with excellent results that has been approved by the FDA. You have many treatment options, Jillian. I have no doubt you'll practice medicine for many years yet."

She couldn't even recall what she'd said to him, had no doubt promised to make an appointment in the clinic to see him, before disconnecting from the call and bursting into tears.

To make matters worse, she lied to Alec.

She didn't have a cold. She was sick to a certain degree, sick at heart. Because she knew the right thing to do was to break off her relationship with Alec now, before it was too late, for Shannon's sake.

Her eyes filled with tears again as she imagined Alec and Shannon at his parent's barbecue.

Who was she kidding? It was already too late.

She loved him. Loved being a part of his and Shannon's life. But she knew full well Alec had no idea what it would be like to share his life with someone who is only going to get weaker and weaker, to the point she'd be dependent on him to help her get out of bed and go to the bathroom.

She squeezed her eyes shut, imagining Alec's green eyes filled with pity. Imagined Shannon's distress.

No, she couldn't do it.

She refused to become a burden to the ones she loved.

CHAPTER THIRTEEN

Jillian dodged Alec's phone calls over the rest of the weekend, but each time she did, she realized she couldn't avoid him forever. For one thing, he lived too close, just on the other side of the park. For another, he was too stubborn to give up without seeing her in person. She expected him to show up on her doorstep at any moment, but he didn't.

At least not yet. But it was only a matter of time.

While it hadn't been easy, she'd used the weekend to pull herself together. She'd grieved for the lost family she might have had with Alec, but finally managed to stop crying long enough to focus on her future. She refused to walk around in a constant state of depression. Her life wasn't over, not by a long shot. In fact, the more she thought about it, the more she realized maybe it was time to consider a career change.

She loved the variety of emergency medicine but had begun to think she should specialize in neurology instead. The idea of dedicating her life to research benefiting multiple sclerosis made her feel as if she might have some control over her illness. After searching various medical websites to gather information and multiple sclerosis, she grew impressed with the various treatment options that were available. Dr. Juran hadn't been kidding when he'd mentioned the new medication regime. The stories of people who had overcome their MS symptoms, to do fifty-mile bike rides or to compete in sprint triathlons, were amazing.

If they could do it, she could, too. All she needed to do was to maintain a positive outlook on life.

Which was easier to do if she didn't think about losing Alec. And Shannon.

She dragged herself out of bed earlier than usual on Monday morning, hoping to complete her three-mile run in the park without running into Alec and Shannon. Quarter to eight o'clock in the morning wasn't exactly early, unless you took into account that her body was accustomed to second shift hours.

She was closing in on the last mile when she saw Alec and Shannon come out of their house, Daisy in tow. They saw her at the same moment and Shannon broke away from her father's side, running toward her with Daisy barking excitedly at her heels.

"Jillian! Wait up! We want to walk with you."

She bit down on her lower lip, hoping she could do this without breaking down. "I'm sorry, I can't stop, I'm running late. See you later." Without slowing her pace at all, she kept right on going.

The flash of hurt in Shannon's gaze tore at her heart and she stumbled, almost giving in to the need to stop and beg forgiveness. Hardening her heart, knowing the pain Shannon felt now would be far less than if she dragged this on longer, Jillian lengthened her stride and ran faster than usual the rest of the way home.

As she emerged from the shower, she heard her cell phone ring and knew the caller was Alec even before she saw his name flash on the screen. When she didn't answer, he left a message.

"Jillian, please call me when you have a minute. I tried to explain to Shannon why you wanted to finish your run, but I'm afraid her feelings are hurt. Maybe we can meet in the park before work, so Shannon knows your brush-off wasn't personal." There was a hint of accusation underlying his tone.

And she didn't blame him for that. She hesitated, unsure of what to do.

With a trembling finger, she pushed the delete button, eliminating the message without calling him back.

"DADDY, I don't think Dr. Jillian likes us anymore."

The expression of utter dejection in his daughter's face rekindled the simmering anger Alec felt toward Jillian.

She hadn't called him back. She was avoiding him and avoiding Shannon. Worse, he didn't understand why.

If he hadn't seen Jillian's brush off with his own eyes, he wouldn't have believed it. It was one thing to give him the cold shoulder, but to be so cruel to a six-year-old especially one who'd put her up on a pedestal, was unforgivable.

He forced a smile. "Hey, munchkin, don't worry about Dr. Jillian. I think she's just really busy right now. We're having fun without her, aren't we?"

"I guess." Her less than enthusiastic response as she ideally plucked blades of grass, wasn't reassuring. Her tiny brow furrowed in a frown as she glanced up at him. "Did you do something to make her mad, Daddy?"

Nothing that he was aware of. If anyone had the right to be mad it was him. And this was why he hadn't wanted to get involved in a relationship. He'd crushed his promise of not creating havoc in Shannon's life by bringing Jillian into their inner circle, and that had been a huge mistake. His daughter had been through so much she didn't need to be hurt like this. He could ignore his own pain, but not Shannon's.

"Sweetheart, let's not worry about Dr. Jillian." He reached over to take Shannon's hand in his. "We are a father daughter team, aren't we? We're the A-Team, right?"

A reluctant smile curved her lips. "Right." Just then the dog climbed into her lap and licked her chin, making her laugh. "But don't forget Daisy. She's part of our team, too."

"Absolutely. I'll never forget Daisy," Alec agreed. The conversation moved on to school, shopping and Bethany's birthday party coming up in a few weeks, but even though he was relieved to see Shannon smile, he's silently vowed to see Jillian in person, to figure out the motive behind her behavior. And yes, to let her know he did not appreciate how she hurt his daughter.

As he dressed in his uniform for work, the memory of the romantic dinner they'd shared at DiCarlos' flashed in his mind. Their date had been the highlight of his month, and he'd really thought they might have a future together. The way Jillian had turned her back on him and his daughter was incomprehensible.

Rudely shoving thoughts of Jillian aside, he clipped his handcuffs into the holder on his belt and secured his weapon. He and Rafe were heading out to arrest a kid by the name of Nelson Collins. So far, the few football players who had come forward had named this Nelson Collins as the supplier of the percocets. Which was odd because from what he and Rafe could tell, Nelson didn't have a contact inside the hospital.

The drugs had to be coming from someone with access inside the hospital, which narrowed their list down to Eric Hanover, Lacy's younger brother, or Gerald Green, Susan's son. Both nurse's names were at the top of their suspect list. They had more interactions in the medication dispensing machine than anyone else. But that was not proof that either of them had shoved medication into their pockets.

Still, his gut told him they were on the right track. If all went well, they would have this case closed by the end of their shift.

Thank heavens he could occupy his mind with something other than Jillian's betrayal.

"Daddy?" Shannon called out as he prepared to leave.

"Yes?" He turned to his daughter.

She jumped up from the table and rushed over to him. "I need a hug."

He lifted Shannon into his arms, his throat thick with emotion as she clung to him. He held her close for a long minute, smoothing a hand down her shiny brown hair.

"Hey, what's the matter?"

"Nothing," she mumbled against his shoulder. "I love you, Daddy."

"I love you, too." He put her down with regret. This past weekend he'd talked to Shannon about his job and she'd seemed fine afterwards. Maybe his daughter was still upset over Jillian. He wished he could stay home with her, but he couldn't. "I'll see you in the morning, okay?"

She nodded, her expression solemn. "Be careful, Daddy."

"I will." He left the house, waving at Shannon as she watched him from the doorway. It wasn't until he'd radioed in and made arrangements to meet Rafe to discuss their upcoming arrest warrant for Nelson Collins that his brain registered just how worried Shannon had seemed.

Maybe she wasn't as okay with his job as he thought. The comments Jillian had made about changing his career for Shannon's sake came back in a rush. He liked being a cop. He was good at being a cop.

Yet as much as he tried, he couldn't erase the image of his daughter's face peering at him from the doorway.

JILLIAN DROVE TO WORK, hoping the emergency department would be busy enough to keep her mind occupied. Because despite the way she deleted the message, Alec's accusing tone slipped into her subconscious so she heard his words over and over again.

Shannon's feelings were hurt. Call me. Shannon's feelings were hurt.

She sighed, knowing she needed to talk to Alec face to face. To let him know why their relationship was over. He might not understand, but eventually, hopefully, he'd learned to forgive her.

And to forget her?

The idea of Alec finding someone else to share his life with caused a rare surge of jealousy to clench in her belly. She quickly thrust it aside. Of course he deserved to share his life with someone. To have a family, more children, with a woman who could be a true partner in every way.

Too bad she couldn't be that person.

She headed into the emergency department with a determined stride. Here at least, amidst the chaos, she was comfortable. In charge.

After locking her purse in her office, she headed into her assigned team, her attention centered on the electronic census board, with a full listing of patients. That answered the question of whether or not she'd be busy enough to forget Alec, she thought wryly.

Someone bumped into her from behind. She turned, catching a glimpse of Lacy.

"Sorry, Jillian," Lacy murmured.

"Are you okay?" She frowned because Lacy looked as if she'd been crying.

The charge nurse shook her head. "Daniel died this morning."

Daniel had died. She closed her eyes on a wave of grief. No wonder Lacy was upset. "I'm so sorry to hear that."

"I have to go," Lacy appeared half dazed. "I can't—I have to leave."

"Take care of yourself. We'll talk more tomorrow."

Lacy nodded and quickly walked toward the staff lock room.

Jillian knew that Lacy, along with everyone else in the department, was still on edge, although it had been several days since the last narcotic theft. Jillian glanced over, nearly groaning out loud when she saw Wayne Netter striding toward her.

"We have a full house. Do you think you can handle it?" He asked. "Or do you want me to stay?"

She'd rather work alone than with Wayne so she shook her head. "I'll be fine. Any patients in particular I need to know about?"

"All of them." He turned to the census board and quickly ran down the list of patients, telling her in detail what needed to be done. The man had a personality of a toad, but he obviously knew his stuff as far as emergency medicine was concerned.

"Thanks," she said when he'd finished. "I appreciate the update."

Wayne nodded and turned to leave. Amy, another charged nurse, stood by the narcotic dispensing machine and called her name. "Dr. Davis?"

"Yes? What is it?" With a sinking feeling in her gut, Jillian hurried over.

"Eighteen percocets are missing." Amy's face was red as she met Jillian's gaze. "And you're listed as the person who removed them."

"What? That's impossible." She'd only been in the department for a half hour. And she'd had been nowhere near the narcotic dispensing machine. She reached over and snatched the narcotic discrepancy notice generated by the machine. "Let me see that."

There it was, and clear bold print, her name and the starting percocet count of eighteen, with the final count of zero.

"I don't understand," she said more to herself than to Amy. The time of the transaction was listed as three-fifteen in the afternoon, and it was three-thirty now. "I haven't logged into the narcotic dispensing machine. I just got here. I spoke to Lacy briefly and then I got report from Dr. Netter."

"Is there a problem?" Wayne sauntered over and for a brief moment she wondered if he'd done this to her. If he'd gone so far as to frame her for the thefts just to discredit her and take over the role of medical director.

"Yes, there's a problem. Someone used my password to take percocets from the machine." Jillian worked hard to sound professional, but the way Amy skirted her gaze made her stomach knot. Did the nursing staff really think she had done this? How could this have happened? Then she recalled Alec telling her he could see her enter her password. She had changed it since then and had been more careful, but apparently she had not been careful enough. Her heart sank.

"I have to report this," Amy said, reaching for the phone.

Glued to the spot, Jillian couldn't move. Not even when Amy informed her that Rose Jenkins and the director of security were on the way. Not even when Chris the medical director arrived, his bushy eyebrows pulled together in a deep frown.

After she'd been questioned for almost an hour, and her office and car searched, the leadership team still didn't look convinced of her innocence.

They hadn't found anything, no proof of her culpability. She tried to take solace in that, but her relief was short lived.

Chris stepped forward. "Jillian, I think we need to suspend you from duty while we investigate this situation."

"Why? We know this person has been stealing passwords." She glanced at the somber faces of the hospital administrators surrounding her. "Do you want me to give you a urine sample so you can test for drugs? Because I will."

"That would help," her boss admitted. "Jillian, I'm sure you understand our position. We'll need to inform the police and let them take it from here, and I think it would be better for everyone if you took a few days off." Chris turned to where Wayne hovered just outside the conference room doorway, blatantly listening as he pretended to help cover patients. "Wayne, will you assume the role of interim medical director? I also need you to cover Jillian's shift."

"Of course." Wayne didn't go as far as to smile, but the gleeful light in his eyes was enough. "Don't worry about a thing."

Jillian couldn't think of anything to say in her defense. Submitting to the humiliating process of giving a urine sample was the worst. Once she'd finished, the two security guards who'd searched her desk, her purse, and her car accompanied her along the route back to the emergency department.

"Wait. I need my purse from my office," she said in a low voice.

The two security guards hovered in the doorway as she entered the small space. She stood there for a moment, wondering what would happen to her. Where could she go? What could she do? As much as she wanted to call Alec, she shied away from that idea, knowing he wouldn't be thrilled to hear from her.

Especially not under these circumstances.

The security guards sent her curious side-long looks. Did they think she was going to go off the deep end, do something completely irrational?

They didn't find the drugs because she didn't have them. Someone else did.

Being alone had never been so hard. She needed someone to talk to. Someone other than Alec. Lacy? Maybe. After all she'd been to Lacy 's house once for a house warming party. And the charge nurse didn't live too far. Lacy was upset, but so was she. They could console each other. And she also wondered if Lacy would remember if anyone else had been around the narcotic dispensing machine during the timeframe in question.

When she arrived at Lacy's house, she noticed the nurse lugging a suitcase to her car parked in the driveway.

After parking on the road, Jillian pushed out of the driver side door, and called out, "Lacy? Do you have a minute? I really need to talk."

Lacy's gaze darted to the street behind her. "No, I'm sorry. You caught us as we're getting ready to leave. My brother and I are going out of town."

They were? On a Monday? "Just a few minutes? Please? This time it was my password used to steal narcotics."

Instead of being shocked and horrified, Lacy tossed the suitcase into the back seat and shut the door. "Don't worry, you have an excellent reputation, Jillian. There isn't a single person there who will believe you're taking drugs."

"Are you kidding? That's not true. I've been suspended. This is serious, Lacy."

"I know it's serious." Lacey's eyes filled with tears. "I can't talk about this now. You don't understand. I have to go. I have to take Eric and go."

As Lacy became more and more agitated, Jillian began to understand what was happening. Seconds later a police car pulled up in front of the house, blocking the end of the driveway. A quick glance proved she was right. Alec and Rafe were there.

Lacy was the one who'd taken the drugs.

CHAPTER FOURTEEN

Alec couldn't believe Jillian was there, talking to Lacy. He tried to tell her with his gaze to step back and get out of the way, but she didn't move. It was as if her feet had been fused to the cement.

"Lacy, it's over." He tried to keep his tone non-threatening, especially because Lacy looked as if she might bolt. "We've arrested Nelson Collins and he told us he obtained the percocets from your brother Eric. Which he in turn, got from you. We had you at the top of our suspect list because of how frequently you used the narcotic dispensing machine. And one of your coworkers thought she saw you placing percocets in your scrub pocket."

To his surprise, Jillian rounded on him. "Alec, there must be something we can do. I'm sure there's a reasonable explanation for Lacy's behavior."

"She's right." Lacy's eyes filled with tears. "Eric didn't want to give Nelson the drugs. Nelson forced him. He threatened to hurt Eric if he didn't cooperate."

Alec silently conceded that may have happened.

During their interview with Nelson he was quick to point the blame at Eric. Of course the guy had not admitted to blackmailing or threatening anyone. Still, it would be nice to have proof. "You're sure Nelson was blackmailing Eric to getting the drugs?" He kept talking, while maneuvering around Jillian to get her out of the way, but she was not helping.

"Nelson stole the percocets from Eric the first time." Lacy crossed her arms over her chest as if she were cold. It seemed that now that she'd started talking, she couldn't stop. "I took them for Eric, only because he was injured. Not to sell." Her eyes flicked to Jillian, pleading for understanding. "Our mother just lost her job just after we moved here and we were broke. I wanted to help Eric get a scholarship. But then Nelson saw Eric taking them and forcefully took the remaining pills from my brother. Then Nelson threatened to get us all in trouble if he didn't get more narcotics. I didn't know what to do. Eric is one of the best players on the team." Her shoulders slumped in defeat. "I just didn't know what to do."

"It's going to be okay, Lacy." When Jillian stepped toward the nurse, Alec grabbed her arm. The woman had flat out admitted to stealing narcotics. They would have to sort out the truth from the lies later. For now, he didn't want Jillian to get in the way of their arrest. She tried to shake off his arm but he held on tight. "I promise, Lacy. We'll find a way out of this. I'll help you."

Tears spilled down Lacy's cheeks. "I'm sorry I framed you, Jillian. I needed time to get away. When Daniel died, I knew I couldn't do this anymore. I never suspected anyone would believe you were guilty. I just couldn't find a way out..."

Alec felt bad for Lacy, but he couldn't let that stop him from taking her in. He hadn't known about Jillian being framed for the theft. Yet it didn't seem as if Jillian harbored a grudge against her colleague.

Rafe stepped around them and approached Lacy. Before the nurse realized what was happening, his partner had both of her wrists pulled behind her back and handcuffs snapped around them. "You'll need to come down to the station with us. I am sure if you cooperate, the judge may go easier on you."

Lacy didn't put up a fight. In fact, she looked completely defeated.

A movement caught Alec's attention and he noticed Eric had stepped out of the front door of the house. He kicked himself for not asking Lacy to bring her brother out here. He dropped Jillian's arm and stepped forward, keeping Lacy and Jillian behind him.

"Let my sister go!" Eric shouted.

"Stay back," Alec warned. He took another step forward, willing Rafe to get Lacy into the squad. With an abrupt movement Eric pulled a gun from behind his back and aimed it directly at Alec.

He froze. He could have reached for his own weapon, but feared that would only make Eric do something drastic. This kid was a football player, not a gang member. Taking a slow breath, he kept his hands up where the kid could see him. "The violence stops here, Eric. Don't make this worse than it needs to be. I promise we will let your sister go if you drop the gun."

"Eric! Don't do this!" Lacy broke into sobs. "Stop, please, put the gun down."

"You heard your sister." Alec slowly, carefully edged closer to the boy, praying Eric might not notice. "Put the gun down, Eric. We will keep you safe from Nelson. No one needs to get hurt, here."

"He's right. It's over," Lacy said, pulling herself together for her brother's sake. Eric stared at his sister as if unsure what to do. "Please, Eric. It's over," she repeated.

"I can't go to jail." Slowly, he raised the gun. Alec knew what he was about to do before the barrel got close to his temple.

"No!" He rushed forward, grabbing the gun pulling it away from the teen's head. But Eric didn't let go. They wrestled for a moment and just when he thought he'd gotten control of the weapon, the gun went off, two shots in rapid succession.

A flash of pain blinded him, blazing a fiery path across his chest and down his leg.

His last conscious thought was of his daughter.

Shannon.

JILLIAN WATCHED the events unfold as if in slow motion. Upon hearing the sound of gunfire, her heart lodged in her throat. Had Eric been shot?

But then she saw Alec's body going limp, falling to the ground.

"No! Alec!" Hardly realizing she was screaming his name, she bolted forward. In some corner of her mind, she heard Eric crying in the background and Rafe kicking the gun away and calling on his radio for backup, letting the dispatcher know there was an officer down.

She worked instinctively, ripping his uniform shirt open, searching for wounds. Instead of finding flesh and blood, she found the surface of a Kevlar vest.

For a moment she closed her eyes in relief. But then realized Alec was still unconscious. Had the bullet managed to penetrate the Kevlar? She felt along the thick material, finding a crease across the Kevlar made by the path of a bullet. Understanding the force of being shot in the chest at close range was enough to stop his heart, she checked for a pulse. It was there, faint and too fast. Intent on taking the vest off so she could examine the skin underneath, she belatedly noticed a dark wet stain on his uniform, along his upper thigh. With a sinking feeling, she touched the stain and looked down at her fingertips.

Blood.

No. Dear, Lord, please...

Understanding Alec had been hit below the vest, she quickly unbelted his pants and shoved the material out of the way to assess the damage. There was so much blood, she knew his femoral artery must have been hit.

Balling up Alec's uniform shirt she pressed it over the seeping wound, leaning on her hands with all of her weight to help slow the blood loss.

"The paramedics are on the way," Rafe said reassuringly. She glanced up at him, noting he'd gotten both Lacy and Eric in handcuffs. They were sitting side by side in the back of the squad. She couldn't worry about Lacy anymore, not now. Her attention was riveted on Alec, who was losing blood at a brisk pace.

Please Lord, save Alec's life, she silently begged as she waited impatiently for the paramedic unit to arrive. Alec needed blood and fluids as soon as humanly possible.

And if they were to save his leg, he'd need surgery as well.

But there was nothing she could do without help.

Without supplies. She never felt more helpless in her entire life.

Her faith crumbled as she silently begged. *Don't die, Alec. Shannon needs you. I need you. Don't die. Please, don't die...*

WHEN THE PARAMEDIC unit finally arrived, Jillian continued to hold pressure as the two paramedics started large bore IV's in both of Alec's arms. She directed them, even though they knew what to do.

"Please secure an airway. Hang the fluids wide open. Get him on the heart monitor."

As she continued to hold pressure, the paramedics followed her commands, then removed Alec's vest. She could see the skin was badly bruised, but nothing had penetrated his chest. Then they asked her to let up on the bullet wound in his leg so they could examine the arterial bleed.

Throughout the interminable waiting, Jillian let up on the pressure every few minutes to help encourage some profusion of Alec's leg. Saving his life was the first priority, but if there was also a way to save his leg, she intended to do it.

The older paramedic wanted to use a mechanical pressure device, but Jillian shook her head. "Manual pressure is better. And it's easier with manual pressure to remember to let up long enough to perfuse his limb."

When the guy looked as if he might argue again, she pinned him with a narrow look. "No. I'm the doctor I'm giving you an order for manual pressure. I'll hold it myself all the way to Trinity Medical Center if I have to."

"Okay." The paramedics exchanged a surprised look, but let the issue go. They took her up on her offer so she held pressure on Alec's leg wound throughout the ambulance ride. It wasn't easy to balance on the gurney, but she managed. Staring down at his still features was difficult. She tried to reassure herself that he was still alive, but it wasn't easy.

"Call ahead, tell them to have a vascular surgeon available when we get there," she instructed the paramedic. "Let them know Dr. Jillian Davis is on scene arriving with a critically injured patient with an arterial bleed."

The paramedic nodded and made the call.

What else could she do? Nothing. Thankfully, his heart was stable, the reassuring beat on the portable monitor helped calm her nerves. Giving fluids wide open, holding pressure and transporting Alec to the hospital as quickly as possible was all they could do to save him.

She remembered that night—had it only been three weeks ago?—when Alec had done the same thing, holding manual pressure over their Evergreen Doe's bleeding chest wound. She remembered being surprised at how Alec had taken the boy's death so hard. He seemed to take his job very seriously, almost to the extreme of doing whatever necessary to save a life. Maybe it was his medic training.

Tonight, grabbing Eric's gun had been risky. He'd saved the boy's life, but at the possible expense of his own.

The screaming sirens echoed in her head as the ambulance rushed to Trinity Medical Center. It didn't take long, and as soon as the ambulance stopped, the second paramedic jumped out, opened the back door and prepared to move Alec inside.

Still straddled on the gurney, Jillian continued to hold pressure as the paramedics slid Alec out of the ambulance and into the emergency department. Wayne would be surprised to see her, but she didn't care. No matter how she felt about Wayne on a personal level, he was a good doctor.

"Is the vascular surgeon available?" Jillian asked.

"Right here." She glanced over to see Dr. Travis Smith. He eyed her curiously. "What do you have?"

"Femoral artery bleed from a gunshot wound. He's lost several units of blood."

Wayne snapped out orders for O negative blood to be given through the rapid infuser. When Travis asked her to let up on the wound, she did.

"We'll take him directly to the OR." Travis quickly agreed with her assessment. "Draw a full panel of labs and let's get ready to move."

William Patterson was already filling numerous tubes of blood. Jillian placed her hands back over the wound to apply pressure. Marianne added blood products to the rapid infuser. Watching the blood being infused into Alex veins was somewhat reassuring.

It was almost another ten minutes, which seemed like ten hours before they wheeled Alec up to the OR suite. When they arrived, Jillian let up on the pressure, awkwardly jumped down from the gurney and stepped back to let the surgical team take over.

She wanted to stay. If she put up enough of a ruckus, they'd probably let her. But she turned away, knowing it was best to let the experts do their job. She wasn't a surgeon, but Travis Smith was excellent. If anyone could save Alec's leg and his life, Travis could.

After washing Alex's blood from her hands, Jillian headed back down to the waiting room in the emergency department. When she walked in, she was surprised to find Alec's parents, Shannon, Andrea and Amber, along with Amber's husband Nick. How they had gotten there so quickly, she wasn't sure. Apparently, Rafe had let them know about the shooting and they must have literally dropped everything to get here.

When Shannon saw Jillian, she broke free of Amber's embrace and rushed over, sobbing. Jillian caught the little girl close and hugged her hard.

"I'm so sorry, he'll be okay. The surgeon will fix his wound. I promise, your dad will be okay."

As Alec's family clustered around her, including her in their group embrace, crying as they offered silent support and audible prayers, Jillian silently hoped and prayed she was telling the truth.

THREE HOURS LATER, Travis came to let them know the operation was over. He was cautiously optimistic that Alec would regain full function of his leg, and that the bruising to his chest and heart wouldn't leave any permanent damage.

Shannon, who had clung to Jillian the entire time, visibly brightened. "I can see my Daddy?"

"Not just yet," Travis cautioned. "Give us a little time to get him settled. He's going to spend the night in the ICU, so we can keep a close eye on his circulation. I don't want to take the breathing tube out yet. If all goes well, we should be able to remove the breathing tube in the morning. And if he's stable enough, transfer him to a regular room by the afternoon."

"Thank you, God," Amber whispered in a heartfelt prayer, clutching her husband's hand. Then she turned to Andrea and Jillian. "We should take turns staying with him. I can take the first watch if you'd like."

"Adam will be here soon," Andrea pointed out. "He was called in to see a patient but planned to come here, afterwards. He'll want to take a turn, too."

"I'll volunteer," Nick offered with a smile. "We have plenty of medical help here to keep an eye on things."

Jillian was humbled by the offers to stay with Alec. The Monroe family was really something, pulling together in a crisis in a way she'd never experienced before.

But falling in love with Alec, with his entire family—especially Shannon, didn't change the facts. She wouldn't impose her illness on them. And this was exactly why. If she were in a relationship with Alec, his entire family would rally around her in a similar situation. Her multiple sclerosis would affect everyone.

Shannon most of all.

It was time for her to leave.

She waited until Adam arrived, looking haggard and concerned, before trying to break away. She didn't get very far, because Shannon ran over to grab her hand.

"Are you still mad at Daddy?" The little girl asked her eyes red and puffy from crying.

"No, Shannon, I'm not mad at anyone." How could she explain why she needed to leave when she really wanted to stay?

"Jillian." Amber left Nick's side to come over, a frown puckering her brow. "We'd really like you to stay. I'm sure you'll want to see that Alec is all right. And I know Alec will want to see you, too."

Her determination to leave wavered. Between Alec's family and the hopeful expression on Shannon's features, she caved. She couldn't leave the little girl now. She'd stay, at least until Alec was safely out of the ICU.

Yet being a part of the close-knit Monroe family, even

for a short time while knowing it couldn't last, would be pure torture.

Rafe showed up asking about Alec. After he'd gone to see Alec, Jillian tugged Rafe off to the side for a private conversation.

"What will happen to Lacy and Eric?"

"They'll be held without bail," Rafe replied. "I can't lie to you, Jillian. The DA's office is pressing serious charges now that Daniel has died."

She closed her eyes, feeling sick. "I know. I just wish there was something I could do. Lacy said she felt backed into a corner, taking drastic action to do what she felt was necessary to protect her brother."

"I hear you, and that is something her defense attorney can explain to the judge." Rafe shrugged. "Keep in mind, Daniel's family will want to see them punished for the role their role in his death."

"I understand." And she did. Maybe Lacy's intent had been to help her brother, but there was no getting around the fact a young man had died. And another had been shot over the very drugs that were taken from the hospital. She had little choice but to leave this in the hands of the justice system. "Thanks, Rafe. I appreciate the update."

"I'll check on Alec tomorrow," he promised before he left.

The night was long, but no one complained as each of the family members took turns sitting beside Alec's bed. When it came to Jillian's turn, she clutched his hand and wished things could be different. Wished she was healthy.

As Travis had anticipated, they eased off on Alec's sedation early the next morning and removed the breathing tube. Alec woke up, seeming somewhat confused to be lying in a hospital bed. She stepped back, allowing his family to crowd around the bedside. They all looked happy now that they could speak with him. Her eyes burned with unshed tears at how Alec cradled his daughter close, reassuring her that he was fine.

A few hours later, they transferred Alec to a regular room. Which would have been Jillian's cue to leave, except Alec surprised her by capturing her hand and tugging her close.

"Please, stay. We need to talk," he said in a low tone.

She nodded, knowing he was right.

Exhausted from lack of sleep, she downed another cup of coffee as his family once more crowded around his bedside. Poor Shannon was practically falling asleep half sprawled on Andrea's lap, so they decided to head home, promising to return later.

Alec closed his eyes for a moment, as if he too, was just as exhausted. After all, he'd been shot, had surgery and spent the night in the ICU. It was tempting to sneak out, to talk to him another time, but knew she owed Alec the truth. He deserved that much, although she knew he tried to talk her out of her decision.

"You were right," he said, his voice hoarse from the breathing tube. At her puzzled expression, he added, "About my career and Shannon. I thought we'd straightened everything out, but after this." He grimaced and shifted on the bed. "I can only imagine how scared she must have been."

"She was, along with your family. I know you value your work as a cop," she said softly. "But Shannon needs you. And after losing her mother, she is going to be more clingy when it comes to you."

"I know." He flashed a lop-sided grin. "I'm taking your advice about moving to something less dangerous. I've decided to sit for the sergeant's exam," he admitted. "It's still considered a frontline position, but there is a lot more desk work and administrative work, too. And from there it's possible I can climb the ranks. I'm not smart like you, Jillian. I've avoided taking the exam for years because I didn't want to be humiliated if I failed it."

It was on the tip of her tongue to offer to help him, but she stopped herself. She wouldn't be there after ending their relationship. "You're smarter than you give yourself credit for," she gently chided. "I have no doubt you'll pass the test just fine."

He nodded and she suspected his motivation to protect his daughter would help him overcome his fear of failure. "During my years in the army I saw too much death and destruction. Most of the soldiers were young kids. I guess I've used that as an excuse to stay a street cop, focusing my energy on saving kids. Maybe I was trying to make up for all of those needless deaths I witnessed."

It was horrible to think about what he'd lived through. No wonder he'd given up his army career to move into law enforcement. And that also explained why he jumped forward wrestling Eric for the gun.

"And what about you, Jillian?"

She frowned. "What do you mean?"

"You've been avoiding me. Us. Me and Shannon. I'd like to know why?"

She swallowed hard, there was no point in lying. "I have bad news." Meeting his gaze was difficult. "Dr. Juran informed me there was a mix up with the results. Turns out my evoked potential tests are positive. I have been diagnosed with multiple sclerosis."

His eyes darkened. "I'm so sorry, Jillian. I'm sure that was a shock for you." He held out a hand, urging her to come over to stand by his bed. Against her better judgment, she took it. "What treatment options did he offer? I'll be there for you Jillian. Whatever they are, we'll face them together."

Face them together. The words almost made her cry. She tried to remain strong. "Alec, you don't understand. My symptoms are mild now, but they're going to get worse. Much worse." He scowled, but she pressed on anxious to give him the full picture. "By the time my mother died, she couldn't walk. She needed help eating and getting to the bathroom. Don't you see? I can't to be a burden to you. It's better for you and Shannon if we just go our separate ways."

"Jillian, I love you." His fingers tightened around hers. "Do you think having multiple sclerosis changes how I feel about you?"

Tears blurred her vision and she tried to pull out of his grasp. "Please, don't."

"Don't what?" His tone was harsh. "Love you? It's too late for that."

He loved her? He actually loved her?

"Don't give me that garbage about your illness. Because I know that if I'd have lost my leg, you wouldn't have walked away."

"That's different," she protested. "You can be independent with one leg. We're talking about multiple sclerosis, a very physically debilitating illness."

"It's an excuse." His eyes glinted with a rare anger. "You're not debilitated now, Jillian. And as a doctor you know there are new medical breakthroughs every day. What if they find a cure for MS five years from now? Ten years? What if I come down with some rare form of cancer? Or something else? Anything can happen. Are you really going to throw our love away because you're afraid?"

Stunned she stared at him. Because he was right. She had been using her diagnosis as an excuse to leave. And hadn't she already convinced herself she had years before she needed to worry? She swallowed hard. "I couldn't bear it if you looked at me with pity. And Shannon—she's already lost someone once..."

"Jillian, sit down." His voice was soft as he tugged her down beside him on the bed. "You can't live your life playing the what-if game. I believe God has a plan for us. It may not be the path we want to take, but it's not up to us to question Him. All that matters is that I love you. And I want to marry you."

"Oh, Alec," she whispered. "I love you, too."

"Thank heavens," he murmured. "You have no idea how much I needed to hear you say that."

She let out a strangled laugh at his blunt honesty. "I love you Alec," she repeated louder this time. "I love you, I love Shannon, and I love your family. I really don't want to be a burden to you, but you're right about my fears. I was allowing them to hold me back."

"And that's not fair to either of us, is it?" He managed a smile and pressed a kiss to her fingers. "We'll fight this together, Jillian. I've learned the hard way how important family is. We can face anything, together."

Together. With Alec's love and the whole Monroe family behind them, she didn't see how they could possibly fail. "We might want to ask Shannon how she feels about this."

"Shannon loves you. And Shannon wants me to be happy. Marrying you, Jillian, will make me the happiest guy in the world."

Well then, how could she argue with that?

"I need a favor though," Alec said.

"Of course," she quickly said. "Anything."

"Please kiss me." He smiled. "It hurts when I move."

She laughed softly, bent over and kissed him.

Knowing this was the beginning of a bright future full of hope and love.

EPILOGUE

One month later...

Alec's parent's fortieth anniversary party was wonderful. The eldest Monroes brought a tear to her eye as they reaffirmed their wedding vows.

Alec had made it clear that he intended for her to be a part of the family sooner rather than later. His impatience made her laugh. And to her surprise and relief Shannon had been thrilled with the news of their engagement.

After Dr. Juran had started her on medication, the numbness and tingling in her hands had disappeared. Oh, she knew that her multiple sclerosis wasn't going away that easily. But being with Alec, had taught her to take things one day at a time.

She had given the same advice to Lacy. Lacy and Eric's case had gotten a little boost when they offered proof of Nelson's blackmail in the form of several text messages. Lacy was still guilty of stealing, but Jillian was confident that Nelson Collins would take the brunt of the fall for his role in what happened to Daniel, Ricky and the others.

Life was good. She had taken the first steps to change

her focus to study neurology. She was determined to help find a cure for multiple sclerosis. Alec supported her one hundred percent, and she was helping him study for the sergeant's exam, too.

Later that evening, she and Alec finally had a few minutes alone to themselves.

"I've missed you," he murmured, holding her close as they swayed to the music. "I can't wait until we're married and living in the same house."

She wound her arms around his broad shoulders. "Me, too."

They had practically worn a path through the park going back and forth between each other's houses. Not staying overnight or anything like that, because she wanted to wait until they were married. And to make sure Shannon was on board with their relationship.

"Are you sure you want to get married in three months?" She thought he'd lost his mind at the pressing to get married so quickly.

"I'd marry you next weekend, if I could."

That made her laugh. She pulled away to look up into his eyes. "I have some news."

"Yeah? Good news?" Alec dropped a quick kiss on her lips.

"I think so." She'd had several doctor's appointments lately that he didn't know about. "Dr. Juran reassured me there's no reason I can't have children. That despite how both my mother and I have come down with multiple sclerosis doesn't mean our children will be affected."

Alec stopped, his gaze locked on hers. "Are you sure? Because I don't want to take a chance on your health."

She nodded, unable to keep from smiling. "Very sure."

"That's it," Alec muttered giving her another quick kiss.

"We're not waiting three months. We're getting married as soon as possible.

"Alec, don't be ridiculous."

"I'm not." His gaze softened. "I love you. And I'll wait, if you want me to. But I say the sooner we get married the better."

"I love you, too, Alec."

"Does that mean you won't make me wait?"

She laughed. "I won't make you wait. Because I want to marry you, as soon as possible, too."

"I'll hold you to that promise," Alec whispered. "No backing out on me now."

"Never." She wouldn't back out. Because she couldn't wait to become a member of the Monroe family.

I HOPE you enjoyed Alec and Jillian's story in *Crushed Promises*. Are you ready for Adam and Krista's story in *Holiday Haven*? Click here!

DEAR READER

Over twenty years ago I wrote a medical based series about the Monroe family. I've recently updated these stories and have decided to re-issue them now. I realize these are not my typical Christian romantic suspense books but I hope you enjoy them anyway. Thanks for reading Alec's story. I have Adam's story releasing in December and then Austin's story in January. I hope you give the rest of the Monroe books a try.

Anyone choosing to purchase eBooks or audiobooks directly from my website will receive a 15% discount by using the code **LauraScott15**. I usually have all my new books available there first, before they are released on other vendor sites. Perfect for readers who don't want to wait!

I adore hearing from my readers! I can be found through my website at https://www.laurascottbooks.com, via Facebook at https://www.facebook.com/LauraScott Books, Instagram at https://www.instagram.com/laurascott books/, and Twitter https://twitter.com/laurascottbooks. Also, take a moment to sign up for my monthly newsletter to learn about my new book releases! All subscribers receive a free novella not available for purchase on any platform.

Until next time,

Laura Scott

P.S. Read on for a sneak peek of *Holiday Haven*.

HOLIDAY HAVEN

Chapter One

Adam Monroe rolled his shoulders and bent his head from side to side, working the crook out of his neck, trying to hide the depth of his exhaustion. "Doris, this is the last patient, right?"

"Yes, I placed the infant and mother in exam number two." Doris, his receptionist, glanced at him with a frown. "You didn't eat lunch, did you?"

"No." There hadn't been time. Adam munched a stale cracker as he logged into the last patient's chart. They'd been extremely busy all day and well into the evening but he knew the true source of his fatigue was plain, old ordinary lack of sleep. Ever since the Christmas season had hit, the nightmares of the car accident had returned. He shook off the feeling of despondency and glanced at Doris's concerned face. "Don't worry, I'll make up for it at dinner."

"Maybe teaming up with the public health department to offer medical care to low-income families wasn't such a good idea," Doris said in a low tone. "You're exhausted."

"I'm fine." As one of the founding partners of the private practice pediatric clinic, he was proud of their success. Tuesday evenings were reserved for the public health department referrals. The first appointment was free, and if the patients needed more extensive care and follow up, subsequent visits were prorated according to income level. Which meant basically subsequent visits were pretty much free, too. "We're providing a great service. And besides, you know I'd normally have Phoebe's help with this."

"True." Doris sighed. "I'll be glad when she's back from her second honeymoon."

Phoebe Cooper was his nurse practitioner, who usually shared his patient load, especially the infants. As she was currently off in the Caribbean, celebrating her tenth wedding anniversary, he was on his own.

His stomach growled as he walked down the hall, mentally reviewing the notes he'd seen in the chart. This patient was a two-month old baby, and he mentally prepared himself as he knocked briefly on the door before walking in.

"Good evening, Ms. Turner," he greeted the young mother, who paced the room while holding a crying baby against her shoulder. "I'm Dr. Monroe. I understand Grady has been very fussy and has been running a low grade fever for the past twenty-four hours."

"Yes." Grady's young mother appeared extremely frazzled, as she bobbed the baby up and down, patting the infants back. The distress in her expression made him fear she might start sobbing herself. "He cries constantly. I tried feeding him, changing him, holding him—everything! Nothing works. There's something seriously wrong with him, I just know it."

"I'll take a look," Adam promised. "Excessive crying is very frustrating and can be from something simple like an ear infection or a colic." He maintained a professional demeanor, washing his hands in the sink and flashing Grady's mother a reassuring smile. He wished Phoebe was here to take this case.

"Would you please set him down on the table for a moment so I can examine him?" When she did so, he performed a thorough assessment. He tried to remain objective. When dealing with small infants, the history from the caregiver and the physical exam were the most important keys to an accurate diagnosis.

Grady's temperature was normal, his eyes and ears were clear, no sign of infection. His heart and lungs sounded good, but as abdomen was tense with hyperactive bowel sounds. He asked about the baby's eating habits and bowel movements and discovered Grady's mother was using a dairy based formula.

He handed the infant back with a sense of relief. "He's not running a fever now. I believe Grady has colic. He likely has an intolerance to milk, so I'd like you to try some soy based formula for two weeks. I'll give you some samples, so you don't have to buy any unless it helps." He washed his hands again, while Ms. Turner dressed the baby in his dark blue sleeper. "If that doesn't work, bring him back here and we will try something else. You were right to bring him in to see us. Babies shouldn't cry all the time."

"Thank you, Dr. Monroe." Her eyes filled with gratitude. Sometimes new mothers just needed a little bit of reassurance.

"I'll give you some information on colic. There are some other tricks you can try, like using a baby swing or as silly as it sounds, placing the car seat on top of your dryer while doing laundry. The motion and the sound seem to help settle a baby's upset stomach." He sat for a moment at the computer, brought up Grady's chart, and made a few notes. Then he quickly logged off. "I'll have Doris give you the formula samples, all right?"

"Yes." Grady's mother was already bundling him into his car carrier. "Thanks again for everything."

"You're welcome. Have a good evening." Adam left the exam room, and almost ran into Doris. "Oh, please take some soy formula to Grady's mother."

"Sounds good."

Back in his office he stared at the package of stale crackers, fighting a wave of grief. As a pediatrician, he knew he couldn't avoid taking care of babies. They were the mainstay of his practice. He closed his eyes and rubbed his temple. How long would the past haunt him? To be fair, it had only been a year, but the Christmas decorations surrounding him didn't help. His memories of the past just wouldn't stay buried.

Somehow he needed to find the strength to get through this Christmas holiday. At least he had a warm, loving, generous family to distract him from his guilt.

Time to finish up his documentation and get out of there. He logged back into the computer, reviewing his patients notes. Once he'd made sure everything was in order, he sent electronic copies to of each record to the public health department. Other physicians provided care, too and they needed to be kept up on what was going on.

His stomach grumbled again and, while he wasn't really in the mood, he knew he needed to eat. Fast food didn't appeal, but it was quick and easy and would stop the gnawing in his belly.

Maybe. Unless he had an ulcer.

"Adam!" Doris called out from the reception desk. "Come here come a quick. Someone left a baby!"

What? Adam levered himself out of his seat, heading straight to the waiting area, thinking Doris had to be mistaken. "Are you sure?"

Doris waved a hand at the empty waiting room. Well, almost empty waiting room. "See for yourself. That baby wasn't there thirty minutes ago."

He stared, not sure if his glucose deprived brain was playing tricks on him. He blinked. Nope, still there. A small, crying baby, safely tucked into an infant car seat which had been left on one of the waiting room chairs.

"I'll check the bathrooms," Doris said over her shoulder as she headed down the hall to the public restrooms their office shared with an adult walk in clinic across the hall.

Adam stepped closer. The baby was dressed from head to toe in a bright pink sleeper. Unless the color was some sort of bizarre joke, he assumed the baby was a girl. He gauged her to be six-weeks-old, her tiny face scrunched and red from crying.

A folded slip of paper was tucked between the baby and the car seat cushion. Fearing the worst, he pulled it out and read the words, carefully printed. *I'm sorry but I can't take care of Joy anymore. I love her, but I simply can't afford to keep her. I brought her here because she's been running a fever for the past two days.*

Abandoned? Someone had actually left a safe haven baby in his waiting room?

"There's no sign of a parent anywhere—I even checked the men's room!" Doris planted her hands on her hips. "I can't believe this."

Adam handed her the note. "You're sure you didn't see anyone drop her off?"

"I'm positive. You know how busy we were. After putting the last patient into an exam room, I spent the rest of the time getting caught up my computer work. I didn't see or hear anyone come in." Her eyes widened when she read the note. "I can't believe it! We've never had a safe haven baby like this. Who would give up their child three weeks before Christmas?"

The baby's crying, which didn't quite sound right, grated on his nerves. He had a new appreciation for why Grady's mother had appeared so frazzled. "Pick her up, will you? Bring her into one of the exam rooms. I'll need to assess her."

Doris was already working the buckle on the car seat. The minute Doris lifted the baby against her shoulder, Joy quieted down. "Oh, my, she really is warm."

Adam grabbed the car seat. It sounded like the baby's mother was right about the child's fever. "Take her into the first exam room."

Doris carefully set the baby girl on the exam table. "Do you think she's hungry?"

"Yes. Go ahead and make a bottle from the samples of formula. We don't know when she was last fed. Sounds like the mother has been in a financial crunch." Thankfully he always carried a sizable stockpile of extra supplies in case of emergencies.

Like this.

Doris hustled off, leaving him to carefully remove the bright pink sleeper. Doris was right—the baby radiated heat from her tiny body. When he checked her temperature, he wasn't surprised to discover her fever was high, 103.4 degrees Fahrenheit.

Joy's sound had a barking sound to it. He listened to her lungs not surprised to hear diminished breath sounds.

Could the baby have RSV—respiratory syncytial virus? He needed to do more tests, cultures and maybe an X-ray of her chest. This baby needed more care than he could provide here, in his clinic.

Even taking baby Joy to the hospital, though, wouldn't necessarily help him provide a firm diagnosis. He didn't have a caregiver to give him a complete history. How well was she eating? How long had she had this barking cry? How many hours did she sleep at a time? Too many questions without answers.

"I have a bottle," Doris said, entering the room. "I hope she'll take it."

He hoped so, too. There was no way of knowing if Joy's mother had breastfed her, bottle fed her, or used a special soy based formula. All he could do is hope for the best through trial and error.

Once he had finished his exam, he bundled Joy back into her pink sleeper, fumbling a bit with the snaps. He intended to hand the baby straight over to Doris, she was more of an expert in this area than he was, but the moment he lifted Joy against his chest, she quieted down.

Awestruck, he stared down at her for a long moment. She was beautiful, her dainty features perfect. Tearing his gaze from her tiny face, he forced himself to think like a doctor. Joy's weight was on the low side for six-weeks-old, and reinforcing the mother likely couldn't afford to feed the child. Breast milk was free, but some women struggled to make that work.

"Do you want me to try and feed her?" Doris asked still holding the bottle.

"Yes, please." Oddly reluctant, he handed the baby over, knowing he should use this time to finish documenting the incident. He'd never had a safe haven baby left in his clinic before. Technically, safe haven babies were to be left at hospitals, police stations or fire stations.

Did a clinic count? He didn't know.

The baby latched onto the nipple for a few minutes, sucking eagerly. But she didn't take nearly as much nourishment as he would have liked. Too soon she let go and turned her face away.

"Now what?" Doris wrinkled her forehead and concern. "She didn't drink very much at all."

"I'll take her to Children's Memorial Hospital as a direct admission. Her fever needs attention." He didn't see an alternative. He couldn't do a complete work up here, his clinic wasn't equipped with a full lab or radiology services. Joy's ears had looked clear, but he wanted blood and spinal fluid cultures. "Please get the baby tucked back into the car seat."

While Doris did as he asked, he grabbed his coat. Winter in Milwaukee, Wisconsin, was cold. He searched through his cabinets to find a baby blanket, tossing it over the car seat to protect her face from the frigid temperatures.

Joy began to cry again, the sound only partially muffled by the blanket. He forced himself to ignore the pathetic sound as he hefted the infant seat in one hand and headed for the door.

"Wait—don't you think we should call the police?" Doris followed him through the clinic and out to the waiting room. She looked concerned, as if she wanted to follow him all the way to the hospital. It was on the tip of his tongue to ask her to come along with him, but that was ridiculous. There was nothing Doris could do.

"I'm not sure we can, mothers of safe haven babies are not considered criminals." He hesitated, then added, "I'll check with my brother, Alec. He's a sergeant for the

Milwaukee Police Department. He might have some advice. Go home, Doris. Thanks for your help."

Ducking his head against the cold December wind, his feet crunched on snow and ice as he carefully made his way to his car.

With new respect for mothers who lugged their babies around on a regular basis, he secured the infant seat in the back. It took him several tries to figure out how to get the carrier buckled in. After closing the back door, he quickly slid behind the wheel. His office wasn't far from Children's Memorial Hospital And he let the car run for a few minutes to warm up the engine.

Joy's cries echoed throughout the interior of the car. He gripped the steering wheel, unable to do anything to stop her crying. He hadn't felt this helpless since the accident last year. His son would have been almost six months old if he'd lived. "Hang in there, Joy, we're almost there." Adam glanced at the car seat in the rearview mirror but couldn't see the baby's face. Infant carriers had to be placed backwards to protect the baby from harm. He continued to talk to her, hoping the sound of his voice would help let her know she wasn't alone.

His attempts to calm her were in vain. She was still crying when he eased into traffic, using his hands free phone to call Alec.

"Hey, Alec," Adam greeted his brother when he answered the phone. "I have a small problem."

"What's up?" Alec paused and then added, "Is that a baby?"

"Yeah. That's my problem." Adam sighed. "She was left in my clinic, as a safe haven baby I assume. I'm taking her to Children's Memorial. Would you be able to meet me there? I don't want to mess this up."

"Sure." Alec didn't hesitate. "I need to arrange for someone to watch Shannon. Jillian's at work. I don't expect her for another hour or so."

A flash of guilt nagged at him. He hated dragging his brother from his family. Alec and Jillian were doing their best to make their opposite schedules work. "Don't rush, you can wait until Jillian gets home. See you later." He disconnected the call and pulled into the parking lot of Children's Memorial Hospital.

"We're here, Joy." Unbuckling the car seat was almost as complicated as getting it put together. "Don't cry, everything's going to be fine."

Adam was relieved he could admit the baby to the hospital where he, along with the nursing staff could keep a close eye on her. And it would only be a matter of time before social services and the department of child protective services got involved. In a safe haven situation, there was usually not an attempt to track the mother. But in this case, because the mother made it sound like the issue was financial, he wondered if they could make an exception. The public health department had a variety of programs, as did Children's Memorial Hospital. Maybe Joy's mother didn't realize the resources that were available to her.

He wanted to reunite Joy with her mother. Unless of course her mother was unfit to take care of her, related to drug or alcohol abuse.

Either way, his first priority was to discover the source of Joy's fever.

"ADMITTING JUST CALLED with a new patient. This one is yours, Krista."

"No problem." Krista glanced up from the computer and the chart she was reviewing. Emily, charge nurse for Six South, had taken the last admission, so indeed this new patient was hers. She didn't mind. She liked this unit, where patients were newborn infants up to the age of about two years. She was relatively new in her role, but learned something new every day. "Where is the admission coming from? The emergency department?"

"Nope, Dr. Monroe is bringing this one over as a direct admission. The patient is a six-week-old baby girl with a fever of unknown origin. Put her in bed 618, as it's directly across from the nurse's station."

Krista momentarily froze. Dr. Monroe? As in Adam Monroe?

"Krista?" She glanced up to see Emily frowning at her. "Is something wrong?"

"No, of course not," she lied. Logging off the computer she stood. "I'll make sure the room is set up."

Checking into the empty patient room, she leaned against the wall, trying to calm her racing heart. Over the past six months, since she'd started this job, she'd never had to take any of Adam's patients. She'd seen him on the unit now and then, but so far he hadn't recognized her. He'd simply nodded or said hello before going on his way.

She'd known this day would come, but felt woefully unprepared for it now. Interacting with him after a full year, would be awkward.

Why on earth was he bringing a direct admission in himself? She swallowed hard. Maybe he wouldn't stay long, simply drop the patient off and leave.

Pushing away from the wall, she managed to pull herself together. She went to the supply room to fetch an LP tray, knowing that babies with fevers usually needed a lumbar puncture procedure. When she returned, she set the equipment near a small procedure table.

She sighed, forcing herself to admit that dropping the baby off wouldn't be Adam Monroe's style. He had a reputation for being extremely thorough. Everyone liked him. Nurses had been known to seek his attention.

She couldn't blame them—if circumstances were different, she might have sought his attention, too.

After making sure there were enough sterile drapes in the drawer of the procedure table, she stepped back and tucked a stray strand of hair that had fallen from the from her ponytail behind her ear. There was no reason to worry. If Adam Monroe hadn't recognized her by now, he wasn't likely to. She had grown out her badly bleached short hair and let her natural dark brown color shine through. She'd also had laser surgery for her near sightedness as her eyes hadn't been able to get accustomed to contact lenses. The laser surgery had been something of a necessity. On her second day of orientation, an eight-month-old boy had grabbed her glasses and tossed them to the floor, forcing her to wear the broken glasses for the remainder of her shift.

Regardless of why she'd slightly altered her appearance Krista knew she looked completely different compared to a year and a half ago, when she first met Adam. He had dated her older sister Danielle, the two of them becoming engaged after a short period of time. She hadn't seen him since last Christmas, after Danielle had broken off their engagement and moved overseas.

She'd only spoken with Adam a couple of times, having been away at college for much of the time he and Danielle had dated. Did he even remember she'd been enrolled in a nursing program? Her most vivid memory was of the night he'd come over to pick up Danielle while her Aunt Beatrice had been there. Krista had been concerned when the woman had lost her balance, twice. She'd asked Adam to take a look and between them they'd examined Beatrice, quickly coming to the conclusion that she had a minor stroke.

Those moments they'd worked together had proved she'd made the right choice in becoming a nurse. A good thing, as she'd only had one more semester to go before graduating.

She crossed over to smooth the sheet over the crib mattress. She pulled out an extra blanket and set it at the foot of the crib. Glancing around, she noted everything was ready. There wasn't anything more for her to do.

Except to stand there, anticipating Adam's arrival. Hiding in her patient's room. How pathetic. Hadn't she changed at all over the past eighteen months? More so than her outward appearance, she'd been striving to become more self-confident, more outgoing and assertive.

Enough time had passed for her to get over her secret crush on Adam Monroe.

Danielle wouldn't have hidden in an empty patient room. Her older sister had always reacted a little differently to things than she had. When they'd been shuffled from one relative's house to the other, Danielle had only gotten into more trouble, while Krista had become quieter and even more well-behaved. She loved her sister, had really missed her since Danielle had moved to take a job in London.

"Which room?" She heard a deep male voice ask.

"Right behind you, in 618." Emily's voice was clear. "I think Krista is in there, getting things ready."

"Thanks."

She barely had time to turn around before Adam

walked in, cradling a baby against his chest with one hand and carrying the infant carrier with the other.

For a moment their gazes locked, his mesmerizing green eyes, holding her captive. She almost took a step back from the impact. Instead, she forced herself to stand her ground.

"Krista? Krista Vaughn?" He stared at her, recognition dawning in his eyes. "How long have you worked here?"

Made in the USA
Columbia, SC
27 April 2024

34968295R00113